I0637552

For Those Who Heal

Book 2 of The Three

Shots Series

Jannah Jette

For Those Who Heal

Book 2 of

The Three Shots Series

Copyright © 2025 by Jannah Jette

All rights reserved.

ISBN: 979-8-9998104-5-8

Table of Contents

Dedication

"To my beautiful, brilliant editor:

You're da bomb and I promise you won't have to re-live

book one ever again!"

-My Editor, Adi Gramm

Sorry to disappoint you.

Content Warning

For Those Who Heal contains content that could be triggering to some. This includes, but is not limited to-

Being poisoned

Being drugged

Death

Graphic Consensual Sex Scenes

Abandonment

Prologue

I didn't want to move to Florida, but I was only thirteen when it happened, so my choice didn't exist. It didn't help that I was also the reason we were forced to move.

Colin was the hottest boy in our class. Jet black, messy hair, pale skin, amber eyes that nearly looked like honey, just walking around our middle school looking like a long-lost Cullen sibling. Somehow, the summer before eighth grade, I caught the attention of those amber eyes.

Our fathers worked for the same company. Colin's father was my father's boss, so we ended up at a lot of company parties together. It was at their cookout on the 4th of July where Colin made his first move on me. I was sitting on the wraparound porch of his house. I didn't want to be sitting further down in the yard where everyone else was; it was too crowded, too loud, and it hurt my ears. He came over and sat beside me, grabbed my hand, and we sat there watching the fireworks together. Of course, in my teenage mind, I was planning out our whole future-you know how teenagers are. Everything feels so significant at that age.

Over the rest of the summer, our parents would plan weekly outings for us all. Days out on the lake, baseball games, theme parks, horseback riding, anything you can think of. Every time he would become slightly more aggressive with his hidden displays of affection; pulling me in for a kiss that he didn't ask for, grabbing places he shouldn't. The first time he stuck his tongue in my mouth, I ran away and puked. My mom found me and thought it was just from the roller coasters.

When school started back up, we had a few classes together. I tried to sit across the room from him, but he would convince the teachers to move me to the desk right next to his. One day, I refused to sit by him and after class he yanked me out of my seat, pulled me into the bathroom, and screamed in my face. I vowed that I would never speak to him again and then I told my parents about what all had happened over the previous few months.

That night I heard my dad yelling at Colin's dad over the phone. The next day my dad was fired. Two days after that, my mother's access to the country club was revoked. Three days after that happened, my parents were called by the school nurse to pick me up early after I started vomiting and having convulsions. Obviously, my parents took me to the emergency department where they ran some blood work and found that I had ingested rat poison. I had eaten a cupcake that Colin had brought me that day. It had white buttercream frosting with pink sprinkles, sitting in a pink wrapper. I didn't think anything about it because he had brought some for everyone who usually sat at our table. The following week our house was packed, on the market, and we left Texas.

We tried to press charges, but since I ate the whole cupcake and had no proof that it was what poisoned me, nothing came of it. I am sure his dad's status in the community didn't help our side at all. But you know how it is in small towns: It's all about who you know and who you blow. That is how I ended up here.

So, that's my story. Now tell me yours.

Chapter 1
Avery
One year earlier

"I'm telling you, Doc, I do try. I have been working on getting over my trust and intimacy issues. It's hard to do when every date I go on, the guy runs for the hills when I refuse to eat anything from the restaurant he has taken me to. I tell every single one of them not to worry about feeding me, but some gene in a man's DNA just can't accept that, I guess," I say from the chaise lounge in my therapist's office.

"Do you feel you are ready to try eating at a restaurant?" Doctor Paige asks me.

"If I were, I would have by now. Outside of myself, my mother, my father, and our personal chef-who took years to earn that trust, I still don't let anyone else touch my food."

"Do you feel exposure therapy could be beneficial?"

I scoff. "What, Doc? You want me to ask strangers to prepare food, and then I sit there and stare at it? Or maybe exposure therapy for intimacy, forcing myself to allow someone to be close to me? No way, my friend. Before *him*, I could eat anywhere, and intimacy didn't bother me-from what little I had been exposed to at thirteen years old. But after *him*, I can't. I just can't."

She looks at me over her glasses. "Avery, if I paid you to eat a cookie I baked, would you?"

I let out a guttural laugh before answering her, "You would have a better chance of me cuddling you for money than me eating something you prepared for money."

"Unfortunately, our time is up. I want to give you some homework to complete before our next visit. I want you to do one of two things: either go to a coffee shop, order a drink, and take a sip of it, or find someone outside of your household and hug them. I want you to tell me how it goes at our next visit."

******

"Can you believe her, Lucy? She expects me to drink a coffee from a stranger or hug a stranger. Who in the sunshine state of hell does she think she is?"

Lucy looks up from her food. "Meow."

"Precisely! She is a lunatic. You are so right. 'If I paid you, would you eat a cookie I made?' I would consider cuddling for money."

"Meooow"

"Oh, Lucy, you are the best cuddler and no one could ever take that title from you - not even if they paid me." I cock my head in Lucy's direction. "Not even if they paid me. But, what if...don't look at me like that, Lucy! Let me finish. What if they did pay me to cuddle them? I saw something about this years ago. A professional cuddler or something like that. I can get the exposure I need without having to date and go to restaurants- all while getting paid to do it. Lucy, you are brilliant."

"Meeeowww"

"Ok, only a little more catnip since you obviously turn into a cat genius when you have some."

I put Lucy Fur down on the counter while I grab the catnip bag out of the pantry. Should I be concerned that my only friend in Florida right now is my cat? Probably. Have I told my therapist that I have full-blown conversations with my cat? Absolutely not. I don't want to be committed. But I can't deny that all my best plans come to fruition over our cat chats.

After setting Lucy up for a fun little kitty trip, I head into my office, fire up my laptop, and settle in with a glass of wine for my nighttime reading. Tonight's reading material will be a compilation of websites. My mental handbook of *How to Build Your Business for Bozos*, while I make my checklist of what I need to do to start my new-found adventure. Anything will be better than the receptionist job that I have and hate. This may take a little more effort than I originally thought.

Cuddle my cute ass checklist

- Come up with company name

- Learn how to do background checks

- Make legal agreement form

- Make rules for cuddling my cute ass

- Buy a little black book (maybe pink)

- Come up with cover story job

- Create business email

- Create business cards

- Open a separate bank account for business

Chapter 2
Avery
One month later

"You can do this, woman. Just take a drink. You will be okay," I say, gripping my chest while staring at the coffee in front of me. I am on the verge of a panic attack, but I need to force myself to do this. Everyone is staring at me. Oh man, this is about to go every which way but right.

"Miss, are you okay?"

Without even looking at the stranger, I wave him off. "Yep, nothing to see here, Buster. Keep movin' and groovin'. Okie dokie?"

"Miss, are you sure? Here, for your tears." He puts a handkerchief down next to my coffee.

Who carries handkerchiefs anymore? "Really, I am…."

My words get lost when I stare at the man in front of me. If there were a living, breathing definition of a silver fox, he is standing over me right now. He is tall with tan skin, salt and pepper hair, blue-grey eyes, and large, muscly arms draping from his broad shoulders. Heart-stopper and panty dropper if I have ever seen one. *Get it together, me.*

"Here," he says as he wipes my tears away that I didn't even know were falling. "You are too lovely to cry, let's dry those up."

"Um, thank you. I promise I am okay. Battling inner demons and I forgot my holy water in my other purse."

Silver stranger laughs out softly, "I see. Would you like company so you aren't battling alone?"

I smile genuinely. "Please. Sit down, I'm Avery."

He holds out his hand. "James. Nice to meet you, Miss Avery."

I gingerly place my hand in his. "Nice to meet you as well."

"So, Avery, what demon are we battling?"

"I need to try this coffee, but I am scared. Silly, I know."

He shakes his head. "Not silly at all, changing a coffee order can be scary. Don't want to waste good money on trying something you end up not liking. Take a sip. If you don't like it, I'll buy you a different kind."

I don't know what it is about his vibes or aura or whatever, but the lack of judgment in his statement sets me at ease. Though his assumption is incorrect, I will not be correcting him since his assumption is less embarrassing than the truth. I raise the straw to my mouth and look back up at him. He gives me an encouraging nod. And then, I do it: I take a sip, and apparently make a face because James lets out a soft laugh after I do.

"Why do people drink this? It is disgustingly bitter."

He unwraps a straw and sticks it into his iced coffee. "Here, try mine: iced mocha. It's a guilty pleasure," he states as he points his straw towards me.

That weird vibe rolls over me again. I'm already trying new things, so what's one more? Maybe if I add this to my report to Dr. Paige at our appointment today, she won't give me any more bullshit dares or assignments. I lean over the table and wrap my lips around his straw, sucking up some of his coffee. A moan slips out from how good it tastes. James's eyes darken before he stands abruptly.

"Wait right here, Avery. I will go get you a mocha of your own."

I nod. "Yeah, okay."

I watch as James heads up to the counter and notice that I am not the only one admiring the view. Half of the women in this place are watching him, too. Who can blame them? He glances back my way and smiles at me. *Yeah. Take that, heifers.*

"I hope you like sweet, cold foam; I had her add some to make it a little sweeter."

I take a sip, and my eyes roll back into my head. "Why have I spent so long without this in my life?"

"No idea, Avery, but glad I could convert you," he says with a gorgeous smile.

We spend the next twenty minutes so engaged in conversation that I look down and notice that my coffee is empty. *Wow, Doc won't believe this. I can barely believe this.*

"So, wait, people pay you to come and cuddle them?"

I nod. "Yes, they pay me to cuddle them. I do not allow them to cuddle me; it is part of the rules. I come over, I listen to them and talk with them while I cuddle them if they want that. It is a new business, and I only have one client, but it is mine."

"Are you looking to take on new clients?" he asks.

"I could fit in one, possibly two, depending on the schedules they would want," I say confidently.

"Can I hire you?" he asks, no hesitation in his voice.

I choke on my own spit. "Oh yeah, um, well, I will need some information first. I do require a full background check for all potential clients. You have to read over the rules and sign a couple of legal documents, then set up payment and hourly pay rate. You do understand this is cuddling and talking only, correct?"

James laughs out, "Yes, desperate times call for desperate measures. I understand, and I can do everything you mentioned. I will pass any background check you run; I am an empty nester with an adult child now. Fatherhood was my priority after Jack's mom left when Jack was just a baby. But I can focus on myself now, and I don't know if you know this or not, but dating is so overwhelming these days."

I suppress a giggle. "I absolutely agree, that is why I avoid it. Okay, well, I need to run to make an appointment, but here." I slide him my business card. "Shoot me an email, and we can set up a day for us to get everything handled and get you on the books."

"I will, Avery. Thank you for allowing me to join you. I think we may kill two birds with one stone from today's run in." He stands and offers me his hand.

I grab it, and he pulls me to stand. "You may be right, James. Thank you for going to battle with me today."

The next thing I know, he pulls me into him for what most would consider a friendly hug. For me though, this is a breakthrough of massive proportions. I have not had anyone's arms wrapped around me other than my parents and my best friend, Sandy, since the whole poisoned cupcake incident. No one else has earned that trust, but this guy just speaks to my soul and makes my soul feel safe. I wrap my arms around him, taking in his citrusy smell, hugging him back. Doc will probably take credit for my breakthroughs, but it is all James. I blame him and praise him.

Chapter 3
James

"How is my most favorite princess in the whole wide world this afternoon?" I ask the three-year-old stumbling into the kitchen.

"Gwumpy, can I have ticken?" Lola asks.

I pretend to ponder her question. "Chicken? I suppose the princess gets what she wants."

Lola claps and waddle-runs over to her booster seat, where I pick her up and strap her in. While her chicken nuggets are cooking, she tells me all about her morning with Betty and the games they played. I take over lunch and getting Lola down for her afternoon naps these days so that Betty can get a nap in, too. Lola has a lot of energy and will run you ragged. Betty is like a mom to us all so this is the least I can do to let her catch her breath. By the time Betty makes her way downstairs after her nap, we have about thirty minutes left before Lola should be waking up.

"Why are you wearing such a big smile today, my Jamesy Dear? I haven't seen one of those on you since before Jack left for college," she says in her motherly tone.

"I had an impromptu coffee date today with a lovely young woman. She was a real looker, Betty. Brown hair, green eyes, freckles- just beautiful."

"Well, my word, Jamesy, I never thought I would see the day that you were hit by Cupid's arrow. You have sacrificed your personal love life for far too long, my Jamesy Dear. Jack is out of the house and has been for a while. It is time you allowed yourself a chance to find happiness," she says with a motherly rub of my arm.

"Quit being dramatic, Mama B," I say, swatting her hand away. "I have done just fine. No part of my life was sacrificed. Being a dad was my first priority, and I am so used to being alone that I wouldn't even know how to handle a relationship. Besides, we are jumping the gun here; it was just an accidental coffee date." I make a shooing motion with my hands. "Now get in the kitchen and tell me what you want me to prep for tonight's dinner, so you have a little less on your plate this afternoon."

I need to distract Betty from any more conversation about my impromptu coffee date. As much as I would like to talk more about Avery, I can't divulge too much. She is young, so very young. Closer to Jack's age than my own, and I certainly can't tell Betty that I am going to be paying her to cuddle me. I have been lacking intimacy for so long that I am resorting to paying for it. I am pathetic.

*****

I am hurrying through my house making sure it is clean and smelling good. It has been three weeks since the coffee shop, and I thought that I had worked past my nervousness. I told Avery to park next door at Peter's and that I would pick her up on the golf cart. I asked Peter if my

27

girlfriend could park there for me to pick up, to keep little eyes from seeing us. Girlfriend sounds better than my paid cuddler. He was very understanding. He knows how hard we all work to keep Lola out of adult business- especially after Reed and Gina's divorce.

"Perimeter check?" Reed asks as I drive by.

"Yep. Have a good night, Boss," I say, waving as I pass him.

My nerves are a wreck. I know Reed wouldn't care if I had a lady friend over since my house is a little distance from the main house and Lola wouldn't be exposed to a stranger. That is not why I am hiding Avery. I just don't want him to know why Avery is coming over. Our ride from her car to my house is silent as she takes in the massive yard and surrounding trees.

"Nice place you have here, Mr. Sullivan," Avery says as she walks around the living room and kitchen.

"Thank you. After Jack left for college, I moved in here to be closer to my boss and his daughter since helping with her is the best part of my job. It only made sense to live here," I say with a shrug.

"Makes sense. So down to brass balls or tacks or whatever they say. Let's go over the rules one more time before we get started."

I nod for her to continue.

"I cuddle you, not vice versa. No hanky, panky or spanky. Payments are made up front. This is confidential. If you see me in public, no, you don't. If any of these rules are broken, you are fired as a client. Agree?" she asks sternly.

"Aye, aye, Captain Avery, ma'am," I say with a salute as I hand her an envelope with the amount we agreed upon.

"Good. Now point me to the bed where my magic mending cuddles will rock your cuddle world."

I shake my head and let out a light laugh as I lead her to my room. It is pretty bare; a queen-sized bed, two nightstands with a matching dresser, a chair off to one side, and a couple of lamps. No pictures or décor anywhere. I haven't had the drive to decorate since moving in here a year ago.

"Clothing is not optional, but how much you wear is. Minimum is underwear and shorts or sweats, I have a set uniform I wear, which I will change into now if you point me in the direction of a bathroom."

I walk to the bathroom and flip the light on for her before returning to my room, stripping out of the clothes I was wearing today and throwing on some grey sweatpants. I walk around the room rubbing my hands together and wondering if I made a mistake, until the bathroom door opens and out walks Avery, looking gorgeous.

Her brown hair is pulled up into a bun, hair falling around her face like a beacon, forcing you to look at her light green eyes. She has on a dark green tank top with matching shorts that show off her toned body. I am stunned silent, but so is she. She is just standing in the doorway, openly appreciating my body. I work hard to stay in shape, so I do not mind her appreciating it at all.

"Okie dokie then, get your cute little ass on the bed and pick a side. Let's mend," she says, breaking the silence that was becoming too thick, too charged.

I lay down on the side of the bed closest to the door and face it. I feel the bed dip behind me and her arms wiggle their way under mine. Her hands find and softly caress the top half of my chest. Her nose is against my back and her legs are wrapped up in mine. I can feel her breathing on my back and can't stop the half chub I get just from this little bit of physical contact.

"Am I allowed to touch your hands?" I ask softly.

"Yes, I will allow that. Thank you for asking."

I place one of my hands over one of hers, so small in comparison to my own.

"Do you want to fill the silence, or do you prefer the quiet?" she asks, sending heat from her breath down my spine.

"I am okay with the silence if you are," I respond. I don't add that I need the silence so I can keep myself at half-mast and not embarrass myself by sporting a massive erection just from this little contact.

"Whatever you need, sweet cheeks."

She turns her head and rests her cheek between my shoulders. My breath evens out with hers. I feel her heartbeat against my back as I find myself drifting off to sleep wrapped in her soft arms.

My alarm goes off at four just like every morning. I reach over, smack the alarm, and try to roll over, but only make it halfway. Here, sprawled out across my bed, is my little cuddling koala. Her bun flopped to one side, she is spread out like a starfish, and has drool running down one side of her mouth. I reach out and push the hair back from her face as I admire this gorgeous, hot mess of a woman who is taking over my bed.

"Avery. Sweetie, wake up," I whisper. I don't want to startle her. I raise my voice a little louder. "Avery. Darling, wake up. We accidentally fell asleep."

"Lucille Elizabeth Fur, get off the remote. Never mind, just drag it here. How is it you can turn the TV on but not off?"

I laugh and stroke Avery's hair again. "Hey. Gorgeous, time to get up."

"What the hell did you turn on, Lucy?" Avery begins until she finally opens her eyes and jumps up onto her knees with her hands up like she's ready to box. "What the fuck are you doing in my house? Get out, you creep!"

I put my hands in the air in hopes of defusing the situation. "Avery, sweetie, look around."

She cautiously darts her eyes quickly around the room and then to me before slowly lowering her fists. "Wellllll, this is a first. I am so sorry. What time is it?"

"It's four in the morning. I am so sorry to wake you, but I need to start my morning run and then get ready for work. Let me take you back to your car."

She nods. "Yeah, okay. Hold on. Wow, I have never been speechless before, so give me a second here…okay. I am so sorry that I fell asleep and then nearly knocked your lights out. I promise that this is not a habit, and I will do better in the future by keeping my professionalism in check. I'll just throw on my other clothes, and I will be ready."

"It's usually pretty chilly this early in the morning with the breeze from the water. Here, let me grab you something warm to throw on so you don't freeze on the golf cart," I say as I jump up to find her some sweats.

When I turn back to the bed, Avery is staring at me with her mouth wide open.

"Are you okay?"

Her eyes snap back up to mine quickly, as her hand flies up to cover her eyes. "I am so fucking sorry. I was just telling you that I would be more professional, and here I am staring at that," she says, waving her hand in the air over my crotch. "Not that. You. Oh, I am only making this worse. I should go. I will just go."

I glance down to where she is pointing and realize she is talking about my morning wood that I hadn't even noticed. I throw the sweats at her, accidentally hitting her in the face before turning quickly to cover myself.

"Avery, I am sorry. I didn't mean to throw those in your face. And I didn't even realize... well, you know. Get dressed, I will take you to your car. Just give me a minute. I'll go into the bathroom, ummm, just...just knock on the door when you are ready." I shuffle into the bathroom and mentally berate myself for hiding in here when I could have been like any normal person and chosen to wait in my living room or kitchen. *Why do I lose all common sense with her around?*

I hear the knock telling me it is safe to leave the bathroom, and I slowly open the door. Avery is in her clothes that she arrived in, and my sweats are lying on the bed.

"Sure you don't want the sweats?" I ask.

"No, I don't know how I would get them back to you. I will be fine, I promise," she says softly.

"If you are sure but I could just get them the next time you come over."

She whips her head up to look at me. "Next time?"

I rub my hand over my face. "Yeah, unless you don't want to come back, which I would completely understand."

She lets out a laugh and grabs my sweatshirt. "I figured you wouldn't want me to come back after I fell

36

asleep and then stared at the circus tent you had going on in your sweats this morning."

"Circus tent?" I ask.

"Yeah, that wasn't a camping tent you were pitching. You must be hiding an elephant trunk in there, so circus tent seems fitting."

I bark out a deep and full-bellied laugh. "You should add stand-up comedian to your business card."

She playfully smacks my chest. "Enough from you, Ring Master. Throw on a shirt and shuttle me back to my car."

Chapter 4
Avery

"Look, I know you are mad at me, but it was truly an accident. I didn't plan to fall asleep. The quiet room and the thud of his heartbeat just like…put me in a place of meditation or something. One minute I was making my mental grocery list, the next my brain was just quiet, and then I was out, I guess," I explain, arms waving around in the air like a mad woman.

"Mrrrrreow"

"Seriously, no guilt trips here. Besides, I have to tell you the juicy part," I say as Lucy moves to settle into my lap for her morning pets. "So not only is he drop-dead sexy, but his muscles are also stacked. He could easily bench press us both. And his dick has to be like 3 feet long. Okay, that is an exaggeration, but I would say a solid seven to eight inches."

"Meowww"

"No, I didn't see it, Lucy! You perv! It was covered. My eyes are still just as virginal as everywhere else, thank you very much. But can we discuss the fact that I was able to sleep next to someone?"

Lucy stands, turning her butt to my face before walking away.

"Fine, I'll save it to tell Doc about at our appointment next week," I holler down the hallway towards Lucy.

I grab my custom stationery set to check in with Sandy. She is my only real friend and I hate that she is still in Texas with that douche of a boyfriend. Every time we have made plans for her to visit here, something always comes up. *"Tim has a work thing I have to attend with him, Tim is sick, Tim this, Tim that."* I gave up trying to make any plans for her to come here and I can't allow myself to go back there just yet. While I have made many strides in my therapy sessions, as well as with my own form of exposure therapy, but I am not ready to go back there yet.

As if thinking about that place summoned the devil herself, my phone rings.

"Hey, Mom."

"Avery Elaine, why haven't you called me lately? I have left multiple messages," she chastises.

"Work has kept me busy, Mom. Sorry about that."

"Oh yes, the bartending," she replies with disdain dripping in her southern accent.

"Yep. Speaking of, I had a shift run late last night and need to get to some more rest."

"So, should I expect to never see you again, then? Will bartending take over your life?"

"Mom, that's a bit dramatic, don't you think? I will plan a visit soon. Gotta run, love you bunches."

I hang up without giving her a chance to say anything else. While I love my parents, I am not close to them. I haven't been since we left Texas. My mother, in particular, always made sure to mention how much she missed her old life every chance she had. As if going through being mistreated, assaulted, and poisoned by your first crush at thirteen wasn't bad enough, let's tack on the years of guilt trips like you were to blame for it, just to add salt to the wound.

I don't have time to think about that now. I have some errands to run before going to Theo's for work tonight. Theo is my longest-standing client, well, my only client until last night. He is a retired veteran with severe PTSD and dementia. I stay with him the two nights a week that his daughter works at the gentleman's club to supplement her income. Taking care of Theo and his needs ended up being more expensive than she had imagined, and I am much cheaper than a home health caregiver. Originally, I planned to charge more than I wound up charging her, but after talking to her and sensing her concern, I wanted to help.

Theo and I don't typically cuddle. I more or less help him into bed, tuck him in, sit on the edge of his bed, and listen to him talk until he falls asleep. Every now and then, if it is a really bad night for him, I sing to him while rubbing his hair while he lays his head in my lap. Beth taught me a song her grandma used to sing to all of them when she was little and it does the trick every time. Once he is asleep, I will write my letter to Sandy and then drop it off at the post office on my way home.

******

When I get home from Theo's in the early morning hours, I follow my normal routine after a night on the job. I shower, throw on a pair of underwear and a crop top, grab a veggie cup from the fridge, plant my ass on my couch, and settle in to watch a little of my comfort movie. I am laughing at the people on the screen when my phone buzzes, showing I have a new email.

Avery,

Hope my email finds you well. I would like to chat with you about finding a semi-permanent schedule that would work for both of us. I hope that you can find time to visit twice a week for the next six months, tentatively. I can pay you up front for the full amount and if we cut plans sooner, the rest is still yours to keep. I really enjoyed your mending cuddles and cleaning your drool off of my pillowcases. Hope to hear from you soon.

James

I look at the clock and see that it is nearly five in the morning. James must have just finished with his run. My mind wanders to his shirtless chest, the way his muscles felt under my hands, the soft, barely-there chest hair under my fingers. Add sweat to that? *No, no, control your thoughts, woman.*

Ring Master,

You do know that most normal people are still asleep at this hour of the morning, right? Lucky for you, I am not normal. Right now, every day but Thursdays and Fridays are open. What days would you like me to consider penciling you in for? And I do not drool.

Avery

I clean up the mess I made in the living room, turn off the TV, and head to my bedroom. I should have been in bed already, but oh well. I have no plans for the day outside of an at-home waxing and then a facemask before going to Theo's tonight. Who doesn't enjoy a little pain followed by pleasure? I get under my covers and my phone buzzes again. I should ignore it, but I am interested to see when James wants me to come back.

Avery,

You give me too much credit with a nickname like that, especially since you run this show. You are the Ring Mistress. I am just a clown following your lead. How do

44

Sunday and Wednesday nights sound to you since Thursday and Friday are already taken? That way you still have Saturdays to enjoy your youth. When I see you on Sunday, we will transfer the money to your account. I will pick you up Sunday night at the same place and at the same time. And yes, Avery, you definitely do drool.

James

I let out a laugh. Me as the ring mistress. I like that he understands our dynamics here.

Clown,

Sundays and Wednesdays work perfectly. I will pencil you in. Better yet, I will find a pen and ink you in since this will be for the long haul. The same place and same time work for me. I will be sure to bring your sweatshirt back to you, even though I have to admit; this is the softest and most comfortable sweatshirt I have ever had the luxury of wearing. On second thought, I may hold it ransom for a bit. Just until your money clears the bank.

Short-term hostage situation. And as far as drooling is concerned, pics or it didn't happen. See you Sunday.

Ring Mistress

With that, I plug my phone in and roll over to go to sleep. My dreams are taken over by visions of elephants, clowns, swinging trapeze artists, and one grey-haired, shirtless ringmaster.

Chapter 5
James

Friday and Saturday flew by since I drove Reed and Chris to an out-of-town meeting. When we got home yesterday afternoon, I got a trim, washed my bedding, and tidied up the house. I wanted to make sure that everything was nice and clean for when Avery comes over tonight. I even went and bought some fresh flowers today. I planned to give them to her initially, but felt that maybe that would be out of line, so I stuck them in a vase in the bedroom instead.

I watch the clock and at eight on the dot I jump into the golf cart. When I get to where Avery is parked, she is standing against her car with her purse slung over her shoulder and my sweatshirt swallowing her up.

"I thought my sweatshirt would be tied up to a chair in some basement warehouse by now," I tease.

Avery walks up and sits next to me. "I figured you would want proof of life."

"You're awfully familiar with mob life. Should I be concerned?" I ask with a grin that I can't suppress.

"You know it, sweet cheeks," she says as she throws her hair up into a messy bun. "Now, let's go get our cuddle on, shall we?"

I drive us back to my place and lead the way inside. "Would you like a drink or a snack?"

Avery throws her gigantic purse she just tossed on the counter and opens it. "No, thank you. I brought my own." She sets down a bottle of water with an orange slice floating in it.

"Okay, so I am still new to how all this works. Do we chat first, catch up? Or do we just go straight to cuddling?" I ask.

"It is your time, James, you decide," she says encouragingly.

"So, if I want to watch a movie and have you cuddle me on the couch, that is okay?"

"Only if it's a good movie," she quips.

I let out a laugh. "Fair enough. How about you go get into your comfy clothes, I will get into mine, you meet me back here at the couch when you are ready. You can pick the movie, too."

"Definitely a deal," she says as she saunters off to my bedroom.

I run to the dryer and pull a pair of sweatpants out, throw them on quickly, and turn on the TV. I am in the kitchen filling up a glass of milk when Avery walks in. The outfit is nearly the same, but in pink this time. She plops down on one side of my couch and I fall on the other, pass her the remote, and lean back while she makes her decision. Noticing a glare, I get up to turn the lights down, and come back to find Avery lying down, back against the couch and patting the spot in front of her.

"Come here, my turtle. Let me be your shell."

I breathe out a laugh but follow her demands. Once I am in front of her, she wraps those silky-smooth legs around my waist and her arms over my shoulders. With her head on the armrest, I pull one arm up and prop my head on it so that I am not blocking her view by using the armrest too.

We barely make it a couple of minutes into the movie before Avery starts singing along with the kid singing to the little girl about the dreams they will make. I have never heard worse singing, but Avery is giving it her whole heart, which makes me enjoy it.

"I see what you did here," I say.

"Why, good sir, I have no idea what you are talking about," she coos with a thick southern drawl.

"A movie about a man creating a circus," I say, playfully squeezing her leg that is wrapped around me.

Her legs wrap tighter around me, and she pokes my rib. "No tickling, Sir."

"I don't recall that in the rules," I say as I tickle behind her knee.

Avery is squirming around behind me and giggling as she pulls her leg out from under me, coming around to straddle me so she can tickle me back. We are both lost in laughter and tickling for a moment until the remote drops to the floor and the sound startles us.

Both of us are panting, and Avery is sitting over my growing erection with her chest rising and falling, drawing my eyes to her rock-hard nipples. I lay my hands on the outside of her thighs.

"Avery," I say, breathing just as hard as she is.

Avery jumps off of me. "I am sorry, ummm. I should probably go."

I leap off the couch to stop her from running. "No, I am sorry. Please, don't leave yet. Let's start tonight over.

We can go to the room to cuddle. I will lie there without touching you, Scout's Honor."

"Were you a Scout?" she asks me.

"No, but it seems like the highest form of promise," I say, half-jokingly.

She nods. "Okay, go assume the position. I will be there in just a second."

Chapter 6
Avery

What the hell was that, Avery? Get your shit together. You have rules, follow them. Now, go out there and act like a professional. Good talk, me. For good measure, I smack my own ass for encouragement.

I walk out of the bathroom and find James lying on his bed, wearing a pair of reading glasses with a book in hand. He goes to put the book away, but I hold out a hand to stop him.

"Whatcha reading over there?"

He flashes the book cover toward me. "I decided to reread the Lord of the Rings series. It has always been one of my favorites." He goes to put it on his nightstand but I stop him again.

"Want to read it to me?" I ask.

"You want me to read The Hobbit to you?"

I shrug. "Only if you want to."

He pats the empty space beside him.

I walk around the bed and scoot in beside him where he is leaning against a pillow against the headboard. Wrapping my legs around his, I throw an arm over his lower stomach and rest my head against his chest. I have never cuddled a man like this; this is a level of intimacy that I never thought I would get to. Truthfully, I figured I would die a virgin, an old hag with forty-three cats surrounding me, likely gnawing away at my carcass by the time someone found me. But this is peaceful. I am comfortable. Feeling the vibrations from James's chest mixed with his soft, deep voice while reading, I find myself back into that deep level of meditation.

I wake to a stiff and painful neck, a glance at the clock on the nightstand says it is five. I look around to realize that I am not in my room. *Damnit, not again.* I sit up and grab my neck right as James walks in, towel draped around his neck, sweat dripping down his abs, sweats hanging so low that his V lines are visible.

"Is your neck okay?" he asks, walking towards the bed.

"No. I guess I slept wrong and it's pretty sore."

He throws his towel on the floor. "Come here," he says as he sits on the bed and spreads his legs for me to squeeze between.

I scoot back into him, and he starts moving his hands along the outside of my neck before switching to just using his thumbs. As he is working out the sore spot, I let out a moan in appreciation while opening that side of my neck further to him. I feel his chest pushing against my back with every inhale he takes and I feel his warm breath running down my neck with every exhale. I roll my head to the side a little more and moan again from how good his thumb feels rolling over that sore spot. His other hand moves up to cup my jaw line as his lips fall to the spot behind my ear on my neck.

"I need you to stop making those noises if you want me to continue rubbing your neck, Avery," he says against my skin causing me to break out in goosebumps.

"Or what?" I ask breathlessly.

"Or your neck will not be the only thing I will be rubbing," he says before placing a soft kiss on the spot he was just talking against.

My whole body shudders involuntarily. I feel his erection against my ass and find myself getting aroused. His hands stop their movement, so I turn to face him.

"All done?" I ask.

"For today," he says as he runs a finger over my shoulder, to my neck, and then up to my chin. "Let's get you back to your car. I have to head over to the main house soon."

I nod and roll off the bed. Instead of putting back on what I wore yesterday, I throw those clothes in my purse and slip James's sweatshirt over my head, losing my balance in the process. With my head still covered and my arms stuck over my head, I mentally prepare for impact, but I hit a hard chest instead of a hard floor. A moment later, I hear the crash of a glass and feel a sharp sting in my right leg.

"Let me help you," James says as he pulls the sweatshirt into place.

"I will be fine, thank you," I say as I look down and see a small piece of glass sticking out of the inside of my right leg. "Shoot!"

James looks down to see what I am looking at. "Come here, let's get you taken care of."

He scoops me up in his arms and sets me on his bathroom counter, reaches under one of the sinks, pulling out a little first aid kit, before going to grab his glasses off his nightstand.

"Doctor, will I survive?" I ask to lighten the moment.

"I'm no doctor, but amputation may be our only choice here. Extreme times call for extreme measures. What do I know though?" he jokes.

I smack his shoulder. "Give me those tweezers."

He swats my hands back. "Hush, woman, let me work my magic." He looks up and winks at me.

I lean back on the counter and let him take control. He is crouched down in front of me, one hand holding just above my ankle, the other holding the tweezers. Getting a good grip on the glass, he gives a quick tug, causing me to wince.

He looks up at me with concern filled eyes. "I'm sorry, but it's out. That glass had milk in it last night, so let me clean this out really quickly before I bandage it."

I nod for him to continue.

He digs through the first aid kit, pulls out an antiseptic spray and then sprays it on the cut.

I jerk my leg back. "Did you just spray me with liquid ice? Why does that burn so bad?"

"Don't be a wimp," he says before he softly blows on the spot he sprayed to help cool the burn.

I snap my mouth shut when he looks up at me while still blowing on my leg. He breaks eye contact long enough to open the Band-Aid and place it over the small cut. Still holding my leg, he leans in, places a kiss above the Band-Aid, and then slowly stands from his crouching position between my legs.

I don't know what takes over me; hormones, lust, the horny spirit, but I grab the back of his neck and yank his mouth down onto mine. I have no idea what I am doing, considering it has been fifteen years since my last kiss, but I am guessing by his enthusiasm that I am doing it right. *Snap out of your own head, Avery!*

James slides his hand up and into my hair, gripping it tight and pulling me even closer into him. I can't stop the groan that escapes from my mouth. James grips under my thighs and picks me up.

With ease, he carries me back into his bedroom, turns his back to the bed and sits on the edge. I place my hands on his chest and push him back, still kissing him fervently. His hands slide over my ass and under my shirt. I snap up, still straddling him and grab his wrists.

His hands still against my stomach. "I know that look. You are the ring mistress; you call the shots. All of them," he says, not trying to move a single muscle.

I nod. "I think we should stop here."

"Whatever you want," he says, slowly sliding his hands out from under my shirt.

"Thank you."

I stand, and he tugs me forward while pointing at the ground. "The glass."

"I forgot. Thank you again."

"Come here," he says as he scoops me up. "Your shoes are in the living room, and we have already established that I am not a real doctor."

I lay my forehead into the spot where his neck and shoulder meet and let out a laugh. "I wouldn't say you are the worst, but your bedside manner could use some work."

He pinches my ass. "Next time I will just amputate," he laughs out.

When he puts me down, I want to jump right back into his arms. I like being in his arms.

The ride to my car has me all in my head. When he leans down to kiss me before I leave, I soak in the affection of his soft, tender kiss that does nothing to help me work through these racing thoughts. I have two nights to figure them out, but first, I need to go calm down a cat that is sure to be pissed off at me.

Chapter 7
James

After getting back to the house, I clean up the glass and jump into the shower. My thoughts keep drifting back to Avery. Her light green eyes looking into mine, half lidded and full of want and need, her plump lips on mine. I pour some soap into my hand and start sliding my hand up and down my shaft. Her moans and pants echoing around in my head. I speed up my tugging to match the visions in my mind: Her on top of me, my hands roaming everywhere. But this time, when she stopped and sat up, it wasn't to stop what we were doing, it was to lift her shirt up to show me those perfectly perky tits. That mental image alone has me cumming all over the shower wall.

******

By the time Wednesday rolls around, I am excited to see Avery- not that I wasn't the last couple of days, but even more so today. I made sure to have a fresh set of sheets on the bed as well as new flowers on the nightstand. I bought a soft throw blanket to put on the back of the couch, filled the fridge with bottled water, and sliced up an orange for her. When I pick her up in the golf cart, I notice she is sitting further away than usual. She didn't start with her jokes or ridiculous stories the entire ride back to the house.

After we walk into the house, I grab her shoulder and spin her around to face me. "Hey, is everything okay?" I ask softly.

She looks up at me with the subtlest tremor in her lower lip. "You should never ask someone that question. You may not always want the answer."

I place my thumb on her trembling lower lip. "I wouldn't ask if I didn't want to know, Little Dove."

She allows a watery grin to grace her beautiful face. "I am confused. About you. About me. I don't know."

I pull her into me and wrap my arms around her, resting my chin on her head. "Do you need to work through this alone, or do we need to talk together to help you?"

She blows out a long breath, "Shit balls, James, seriously? Why do you have to be so good?"

"How would you rather I be?"

"Right now, a jerk would have helped me more. You only confuse me more by being so nice," she says as she finally wraps her arms around me.

"Why don't you spill the beans and we can figure it out from there."

"Fiiiiiiiiine, but can we sit down? I don't know how long this will take," she says into my chest.

I nod against her head and scoot her backwards to the couch, not removing my arms from around her.

"James, you are ridiculous," she laughs out.

"Remind me of that if we are ever in a life-or-death situation and our only way to live is to win a potato sack race, not to pick you as my partner," I say, scooting her back a little further.

She pulls back from my arms and swats my side. "I will remember that statement if I ever see you in a life-or-death situation. James, who?"

"Sit and tell me what is on your mind," I demand, pointing at the couch behind her.

With a huff, she falls back. "I need to tell you something before I tell you why I am confused. I think that once you hear it, you will understand a little better."

I nod. "Hit me."

She looks up and then back at her hands in her lap, and in a barely audible whisper, she says, "I am a virgin."

I lean back slowly onto the couch, never taking my eyes off of her while registering what she just told me.

"See, okay, now I made it weird. I am an idiot. Cher, strike me now. I should just go home. I will refund you all your money. I am sorry. I thought I could handle this, but I was so wrong."

It takes me a second to realize that she just said she is leaving. I put my hands in the air to stop her. "Wait, sit down, wait a minute. You didn't make anything weird and you damn sure are not an idiot. I don't want my money back. And if you truly want to leave, I will take you back to your car...but I do not want you to leave if that is what you are thinking. I want you to stay. I want your cuddles, your kisses if they are still available, and anything else you are comfortable sharing with me. This does explain the other day, but if we are being honest, I wrote the other day off as me crossing a boundary and you putting it back in place. Which you have every right to do. I did not think anything was off about that."

"You mean to tell me that I have been stuck in this crazy train of a brain for two days while you haven't given a single shit?" she asks, pointing to her head.

"I have given many shits, Little Dove, many. But none that would have changed my opinion of you in any capacity."

"Ya know what, James? Shut up, put a movie on, and get into turtle position so I can shell you. I am done listening to this sweet poison ooze out of your mouth tonight. You have absolutely no right to be this good of a man. No man does. There is a reason we women say there are no good ones left, and you can't be out here proving us wrong. We are always right. About. Every. Thing." She blurts out, finger waving in my face like a teacher chastising a student.

I throw my head back and laugh. "Yes, Little Dove." I bring her hand to my mouth and kiss her knuckles before following the orders she demanded.

She wraps one of her arms and legs around me. "James, before you press play, I have one question."

"Ask away."

"I don't fall asleep at other client's houses. I don't know what kind of clean-smelling sleeping gas you have flowing through these vents, but I can never seem to avoid it here. Does that bother you?" she asks nervously.

I give her arm that is wrapped around me a squeeze. "Not in the slightest, Dove. I find that I sleep better when you are here. Even when it is sitting up because I am terrified to wake you."

Her body shakes from the soft giggle she lets out. "I sleep better when I'm here, too. Thank you for being honest with me. Now, press play so I can sing along to all the songs the burlesque dancers belt out."

I smile to myself, kiss her hand, and get comfortable with her wrapped around my back. When I notice twenty minutes later that she goes two songs without singing, I peek over my shoulder to find that she is already fast asleep. I carefully slide out from her embrace, scoop her up, and carry her to my room.

She is still dressed in her jean shorts, but I won't wake her to change. I put her in my bed fully clothed and watch her stretch out, leaving me with the tiniest sliver of bed to lay on. I strip out of what I wore today and put on a pair of sleep shorts. When I sit down, Avery groggily rolls off the bed and walks into the bathroom. While she is in there, I turn off the light, roll my back to the door and get comfortable before she comes and steals the whole bed again.

A few minutes later, Avery lifts the blankets and slides under them. She puts a hand on my arm, and within seconds, I hear her soft snores that have become my favorite lullaby.

Chapter 8
Avery

When I open my eyes and see James's poorly decorated bedroom, I am not startled this time. That is until I feel his hand laying on my bare ass cheek. I slowly glance over my shoulder towards my ass, and sure the hell enough, my ass is out on full display. Why did I wear a thong yesterday? I lean back a little so I can tilt my head to look and see if James is still asleep. He is not. His eyes are glued to his hand that is still laying on my ass cheek. When he finally looks up and sees me looking at him, his hand grips me tightly.

"I swear that when I brought you in here last night, you were fully clothed," he rushes out.

I smile and shake my head. "I know you didn't do this, you clown; I did. I didn't bring my normal outfit because I thought for sure you would tell me to leave immediately, and I guess when I went to pee last night, I thought I was at home and got comfortable."

"This is what you wear to bed at home?" he asks, his grip getting a little tighter.

"Well, yeah, it is just me and my cat. Why would I wear more than I need to? I don't enjoy doing laundry."

"Damn, Dove, I need you to go put clothes on. Any clothes: yours, mine, a curtain from the window, I don't care. But I desperately need you to put something over this ass," he states, eyes glued back to where his hand is gripping me so hard that I am positive I will have fingerprint bruises.

"James Michael Sullivan, are you an ass man?"

"No, Dove, I am a *you* man. There is not a single inch of you that I do not want to touch, kiss, taste, and do dirty and despicable things to."

I gasp, but I know I need to roll out of bed before I turn and attack him. I roll off my side and begin walking around the foot of the bed, heading to the bathroom where

I left my clothes. When I pass in front of James, he reaches out and grabs my hand to stop me.

"Can I just admire you for a minute? I promise I won't touch. Just let me appreciate how fucking gorgeous you are before you cover up again."

I nod. "What do you want me to do?"

"Just stand here, turn around in circles, dance around, whatever you want to do. Just do it wearing only this, just a little longer, so I can burn this vision into my memory."

His words awaken some inner part of me that is screaming to sway around and get back in that bed. To allow this man to do those dirty and despicable things to me. I lift my arms over my head to stretch, causing the crop top I wore last night to rise up. I took my bra off when I ditched my shorts, so I'm delivering a perfect shot of under boob with this stretch. I hear a light appreciative moan from my audience, which only encourages me to do more for him. With my arms still up, I slowly turn around and then bend at the waist and drop my arms to the side of one leg before moving to the other to stretch out my legs, giving him a perfect view of my bare ass and panty-covered pussy.

"Fuck, Little Dove," James groans, gripping his sheets, "you are the most divine thing my eyes have ever seen. Go cover up. I am pushing the limits of my own restraint."

I slowly rise, walk to the bathroom, and with the door still wide open, I bend over to put my shorts on, ass still on full display for James.

"Dove," he growls in warning.

I look back over my shoulder and grin while I shimmy my shorts up before I turn to face him as I button them. I decide I want to see what his breaking point will be, so I grip the bottom of my crop top and pull it up over my head so I can put my bra on. Before I even have the bra in my hands, James jumps from the bed and is in the bathroom in two large strides. His hands go to my ribs and he picks me up off the ground. I wrap my legs around his waist and my arms around his neck. He pulls my chest against his as he kisses me with a hard and punishing kiss. His hands spread from just under my shoulder blades all the way around to cup my side boob.

"Avery, you are torturing me on purpose, aren't you?" he asks against my mouth.

"I thought you wanted to admire all of me?" I tease.

He pulls me back and looks down at my tits before smashing me against his chest and kissing me again. He walks us to the bed and softly lays me down, standing over me, just admiring my topless body.

"Can I touch you? Only what is exposed to me right now?" he asks quietly.

"Yes," I breathe out.

He sits himself between my legs and lays his hands on either side of my stomach. Slowly but firmly, he begins rubbing up with his hands meeting under my boobs. He runs his calloused fingers over my sternum a few times before moving his hands over my tits. My nipples are responsive to his touch and it causes a shiver to run through me.

He leans down, placing kisses between my boobs and looks at me, silently asking for permission to continue roaming my body with his mouth. I run my hand through his hair and nod my consent to him. His mouth moves to one nipple and I feel an orgasm building within me. Whichever nipple doesn't have his mouth has a hand playing with it; pinching, light tugs, rolling between his rough fingers.

"James, I am going to cum if you don't stop."

His head snaps up. "Please do, Dove. Please fucking do."

His mouth makes its way back to my tits, my orgasm building higher and higher. I grip his hair when I feel myself about to fall over the edge. A groan slips from his mouth that matches my own. His hands slowly and softly roam over my body as I come down from my orgasm. I never knew that I would be able to cum from just nipple play. Since I am the only one who has ever touched me before, there are a lot of things I have not explored.

He rests his forehead near my belly button. "I can smell your orgasm."

"What?" I panic. "You are lying."

James lifts his head to look me in the eyes. "I am not lying, Dove, I will never lie to you. You smell exquisite after you cum."

I blush and try to roll away, but he grabs my hips and stops me.

"Do not blush and hide from me, you have no reason to have that kind of reaction. Sex and intimacy are completely normal and not shameful or embarrassing. You are a queen, Avery, a fucking queen. Own it."

I sit up, grab his face, and give him a demanding kiss. *Why is this man so perfect in every single way?*

******

"I am not even kidding, Doc. Since our last visit, I hugged, cuddled, kissed- like really kissed- and orgasmed from him. I even woke up with him touching my bare ass and I didn't slap him or freak out or anything. Want to see the proof?" I roll over to show Dr. Paige the fingerprint bruises on my right butt cheek.

"I believe you and don't need visual proof, Avery. How do you feel about the progress that you have made?"

"Well, after the orgasm, I was ashamed, but he told me that I shouldn't feel embarrassed or ashamed. That sex and intimacy are normal. I know that you have been telling me that for years, but hearing it from someone who isn't a doctor made it feel normal. No offense or anything. I never thought I would trust anyone to even kiss me again, and here I am letting this guy diddle my nipples to the big O. Who would have thunk it, Doc?"

Dr. Paige coughs out, "No offense taken. So now that we know exposure therapy is effective for you, and that you were able to drink a coffee made by a barista, do you think you are ready to try food prepared by someone else?"

I feel the tightening in my chest. "I know that on the intimacy aspect, I have been an overachiever and your star pupil, but I'm not ready to dip my toes into that pool yet. I'm not saying it is a hard no, but for now, it is a no."

"That is a good response, Avery. I am very proud of the progress you have made and your willingness to keep an open mind about further progress in the future."

******

Sandy,

You are never going to believe this! I just had my first orgasm that **was not** given to me by me. Didn't think I would still be a virgin at 27, or maybe I did, I don't know. But I can now confirm that nipple play is a yum for me. I know our birthdays are nearly 5 months away, but have you thought about coming out? The water will be a little chilly, but we can handle it. Lucy Fur hates me a little since I haven't been home as much lately. I need an ally in the house, even if it is only for an extended weekend. I will cover the costs for you to come. Consider it half of my birthday gift to you, the other half is me, of course. I miss you, Peach!

Your best friend!

Chapter 9
James

"I know this is last minute, James, but we have an extended trip coming up. We leave Friday and won't be back for a month at minimum, six weeks maximum," Reed says, walking into the dining room.

"Is this an all-hands-on deck or just my boys?" Betty asks between bites of her dessert.

"Just the boys and Chris. I hope you don't mind hanging back, Bets. I don't think Gina could handle being the only caregiver for that long and I don't want to take our princess with us and keep her away from Gina now that we have finally found a good groove."

Betty pats Reed on the cheek. "I don't mind at all, my boy." Betty kisses Reed, then Lola, before making her way to kiss my cheek. "I am off to bed, my loves. I will see you all in the morning."

I kiss her forehead. "Goodnight, Mama B. Where are we going, boss?"

"Don't hate me," he says as he plays with Lola's hair while she colors, "but we are going to North Dakota."

"Well, isn't that just lovely? Same hotel?"

Reed nods. "Unfortunately."

I rub my hand down my face and let out a sigh. "Great. Maybe we will get lucky and she won't be there this time."

Reed shakes his head. "No such luck, she is the client. Sorry, man. I bet you could lube up your cheeks, so her fingers slip off when she tries to pinch them. Maybe then it won't be so bad."

I shiver. "It's not the cheeks on my face I am worried about. I will find some padding to throw in my pants, I suppose."

"Gwumpy, wiww you bwing me a new teddy?" Lola asks, giving me her signature puppy dog eyes with the pouty lips. It is the can't-say-no double whammy.

"Have I ever forgotten to get you a teddy on my travels, Princess?" I ask as I crouch down to her level.

"Not yet, but you cannot dawt now," she says, her little toddler finger pointed at me.

"I wouldn't dream of it. I am going to do my check. Reed, just text me the time to be ready. Lola, I hope you have all the best dreams."

I lean down to kiss her head and pat Reed on the shoulder before heading out the back door. I finally get to see Avery again after having to cancel Sunday. Betty fell and bruised herself up pretty badly, so I took her to the hospital to get it checked out, and we ended up being there all night. Now that I know we will be out of town for a while, I want to hurry and snatch Avery up. I don't want to miss a second of my time with her tonight.

When I pull up to Avery's old beat-up car, she jumps out and skips over before sliding in next to me and planting a kiss on my cheek.

"What was that for?" I ask as I turn around and head back to my place.

"Well, I won't get to see you Friday since I work and all, so it's the beginning of your birthday gift. Excited?"

I run my hand over my face and down my neck. "Honestly, no. I have to tell you something."

She looks my way, nervousness written all over her face.

"I am leaving Friday for work; I will be gone for four to six weeks."

She lets out a soft laugh. "We need to have conversation etiquette 101, Turtle. Never use those words again. 'I have to tell you something'," she says in a mocking voice. "Are you going somewhere tropical? Fun? Please tell me it's somewhere awesome."

It is my turn to laugh now. "North Dakota."

Avery blows out a long breath, "Dayyyyuuummm. That is definitely not tropical, fun, or awesome. Guess it is a good thing I brought you a special birthday surprise to enjoy before you go."

I park and we walk into the house. "And what is that, Little Dove?"

She walks over to the couch, turns to face me, and then unties the dress she is wearing. My eyes follow it to the floor before looking back up to see her in the sexiest lingerie I have ever seen. Her perky tits are covered by the sheerest red lace, exposing her tiny pink nipples with matching panties that barely cover her perfectly waxed pussy.

"Unless, you don't want your birthday surprise," she says as she straightens her spine.

"Dove, there is nothing in this world that I want more right now than the gift standing in front of me. But-

and trust me when I say- this is not a conversation I want to have…but I know that we need to have. Come here; let's sit and talk before anything happens here."

Her shoulders slump as we walk towards the couch. I wrap her hair around my hand and softly pull her head back, walking against her back and leaning down to whisper in her ear, "None of that, Dove. You still run this show, so straighten back up."

She tries to turn to face me, but I softly pull her hair back again.

"Not until you bring my Queen back to me," I say as I run my hand from her belly button up over her breast and to her shoulder, where I push them back into place.

When she stands tall on her own again, I let go of her hair and plop down on the couch before patting my lap, where she obliges me and sits.

"Now, Dove, the talk that we need to have is: What are your boundaries tonight?"

She wraps her hands around my neck and turns to straddle me. "I guess I didn't think about that yet. I don't know how far I will be willing to go yet, but I know that I want to find out with you, and I trust you to stop if I decide that I don't want to go further tonight."

I run my fingertips along her spine. "Pick a safe word. Say it and we stop, no questions asked."

"Safe word? Is that really necessary?" she asks with a laugh.

"Yes, because no matter what is going on, I want you to remember that you are the one in control."

She grabs onto my hair and tugs my head back, "Mahout."

"Mahout?"

She nods. "Mahout. It's what they call an elephant trainer. Mahout."

"Mahout it is, Dove," I say against her lips before kissing her softly.

I grab her thighs and flip her onto her back, kissing down her neck and chest, stopping to look at her for permission. She arches her back, pushing her tits closer to me, and I suck a laced-covered nipple into my mouth, a soft moan escaping her swollen lips.

"James, please don't take this wrong, but this gift is about to be more for me than it is for you," she whispers as she pushes my head further down her stomach.

"You underestimate how much I have wanted to taste you if that is what you think. But keep thinking that this is only for you," I say, trailing kisses down her stomach and enjoying the tautening of her muscles under my mouth.

I trail my thumb down her lace-covered cunt, splitting her lips when I bring my thumb back up, Avery mewling beneath me. I lean down, teasing her through the lace with my breath and mouth. Avery grabs my hair and lifts my head up long enough to slip her thumb into the sides of her panties and start sliding them off. I take over, and when they are on the floor, I start kissing and nibbling up her legs.

"Look at that sight, Dove. Your pussy is dripping for me." I run a finger through her slit before bringing it to my mouth, savoring her taste. "Fuck, you taste better than I imagined you would."

"Please, James."

I lean back down and start licking her sweet cunt, her hips lifting to meet my mouth. When I stick a finger inside of her, her moans start getting a little deeper. By two fingers, she is grinding against my hand on the verge of cumming. She is so tight that my cock is twitching.

"Take it, Dove, own it," I say, pushing a third finger inside her.

"Finger fuck me harder, James, harder," she pants.

I do as she says and then bite down on her clit. Her whole body goes stiff, and I feel her pussy clenching around my fingers. When she has come down from her orgasm, I kiss up her body. Before I can get to her mouth, she lunges forward, pushing me to sit up as she stands.

"I want to make your gift about you now, but I have never done this before. So like, tell me if I suck and I will stop."

"You are meant to suck," I joke. "But I don't think you have anything to worry about as long as you don't bite my dick off."

Avery kneels before me and pulls my sweats and underwear down before leaning over my hard cock. "I did watch some porn earlier. For scientific purposes, of course," she states before flattening her tongue against my shaft, licking to the tip and swirling her tongue around it.

I roll my head back while digging my hands into her hair.

Avery snaps her fingers at me. "Eyes right here," she says, pointing to my dick.

"Fuck. Yes ma'am."

I lock my eyes onto her and watch as her head bobs up and down on my cock, hand pumping in sync with her mouth, making the most obscene and sexy slurping noises. When her other hand grabs and gives a light tug to my nuts, I have to pull her off of me.

"Dove, I'm about to cum."

She smacks my hand away. "It's my show." She lowers her head back onto my cock and starts playing with my nuts again.

Within seconds, I am cumming down her throat. She takes every drop. Her smile as she pulls away from me is my new favorite look on her.

Climbing onto my lap she asks, "Was that okay?"

I kiss her puffy lips that taste like me. "Better than okay. It was magnificent."

"Would it be alright if that is as far as we go tonight?"

"Absolutely," I say between kisses.

"Can I wear one of your shirts to sleep in tonight?" she asks softly.

"Now that you mention it, yes. I want that to be the only thing you wear when you are here from now on."

She smacks my shoulder. "You wish. I'm going to go clean up. Find our movie for tonight, almost birthday boy," she says as she leans in to kiss me before heading to my room.

I queue up another musical since I know they are Avery's favorites and get comfortable waiting for her to make her way back to me.

Chapter 10
Avery

I look at the girl in the mirror and don't even recognize her. That smile, that glow, that power. For the first time in fifteen years, I feel like who I was before that summer. I feel light and happy, like what James and I just did blew up the wall that I thought was permanent. James can sit here and say that I was the one in control, but in some ways, he was. He proved to me, yet again, that I can trust him and I can allow him to keep me safe when I am vulnerable. I hurry to clean myself up and slide one of his t-shirts over my head before heading back to the living room.

"Did you pick this for me?" I ask when I see one of my favorite musicals starting.

"I did. You seem to enjoy singing along to musicals."

"Are you sure this is what you want? Technically, we are celebrating your birthday. Movie choice is all yours tonight."

"Dove, come be my shell and shut up unless you are singing along."

I let out a laugh and shake my head before pouncing on him. "Lay down, won't you be my turtle? Lay down, won't you be my turtle? Lay down, won't you be my turtle? Cuddles from your favorite shell. Cuddle power," I sing off-key as I wrap myself around him.

"Whoever created the theme song for Teenage Mutant Ninja Turtles should have consulted with you before finalizing their work," he says, giving my foot a tickle.

I bite down on his shoulder in warning. "Shush it. Here comes Carlotta, she makes me feel good about my singing."

******

I wake with James behind me in his bed, his arms wrapped around my stomach and chest, legs draped over mine, and his hard cock against my ass. I push my ass back to gauge whether he is awake or asleep. I get my answer when he lets out a groan and buries his face in my hair.

"Don't do this to me, Dove. Don't tease me when I am already dreading going so long without being able to see you."

"Then let me start your day off right and give you something to hold you over."

He ruts his morning wood harder against my ass. "What did you have in mind?"

"You may think it is silly, but I have never had the chance to dry hump anyone, and I feel like it is a rite of passage or something. Could we, um, do that?"

"Anything you want."

James shifts us to where he is on top of me and between my legs. Leaning down to kiss me, he grips one of my legs and wraps it around his back before doing the same with the other. He places an arm next to my head and the other wraps under my hips, pulling my center to his as he rolls his hips slowly against me. I grip his head and pull his mouth harder against mine while I start grinding against him. Even with our underwear on, I feel every ridge of him.

"Come here, get on top of me," James growls out.

I roll with him and take control. I start with a slow roll, and as his kisses get harder, I pick up a quicker pace. I feel my orgasm building, so I add a bounce in with my grind. James grips my ass, thrusting up to meet me.

"You are so fucking gorgeous. Cum for me, Dove, I want to watch your panties drip for me."

His words push me over the edge; I fall on top of him. One final thrust up from him and I can feel him cumming under me.

"I don't want to go," he whispers into my hair that is surrounding us.

I sit up. "It is just a few weeks; you will be fine."

"I know I will, but what will I do without your awful singing for two weeks?" he asks with a laugh.

"Give me your phone," I say with my hand held out.

He hands me his unlocked phone, and I put my phone number in.

"There ya go, now you can call me when you miss my singing. You are one of the few people in the entire world who have phone access to me. Do not take advantage of this privilege. Now, shuttle me back to my car. You slept in, and I can't have you running late on account of me."

He rolls me over onto my back, grips my ankles and spreads my legs open. "First let me admire this gorgeous view for a minute."

******

As we drive over to my car, I feel my heart getting heavy. His words about not wanting to leave mirror how I feel. I enjoy our time together too much and know that the next four to six weeks will be hard on me, but I won't let him see that. When we pull up to my car, I slide out of the seat and walk towards my driver's door, when James grabs me and spins me around to him. His hands grip both sides of my head, and he pulls me in for a deep and sensual kiss.

"Miss me while you're gone," I whisper, his hands still holding my head and his eyes searching mine.

"I already do, Dove." With another demanding kiss, he turns to head back to his place.

I feel like a fool driving home with tears falling, Celine singing, and my chest feeling like cinderblocks are sitting on it. He is a client that I have blurred the lines with. One whom I want to be more with, and I assume that he is wanting the same. I need to sleep on it. Sandy's Memaw always told us girls that if something was eating at us to sleep on it. I have up to six weeks to sleep on it and figure this all out. For now, I need to go home and sleep some more before I go to Theo's tonight.

******

"James, you have only been gone for two days. I didn't think you would miss my singing this soon," I say after I pick up the phone.

"It's Sunday. I'm used to hearing your lovely voice on Sundays."

"Flattery gets you nowhere when you are across the country, James."

He chuckles out, "Flattery is for liars. I miss your voice, Dove. I wish I were home with you watching a movie, laughing about anything."

I blush. "Yeah, yeah, you just miss my mending shell. So, how is it going up there?"

"Boring. Awful. No, dreadful. Our client is this woman who is nearing eighty who thinks herself a cougar, I suppose, because for whatever reason, she has had her sights set on me for nearly two years now. I bought padded underwear so when she pinches my ass, it isn't me she is touching."

I laugh so hard I snort. "No way! You are making this all up."

"I wish I were! I'm being dead ass honest. It is just another reason I can't wait to get back home. How has everything been going for you?"

"Same old song and dance. Lucy is enjoying your absence, or just maybe enjoying my presence. Our conversations are less yelling and more mellow since you have been gone."

"I see. Well, Dove, I hate to cut it short, but my boss just walked in to drag me to dinner with the old grabby crab. Call you on Wednesday. I miss you," he says solemnly.

"Well, miss me some more between now and then. Don't replace me with the molesting matron," I quip.

"Never, Little Dove."

******

"Lucy, we have hit the month mark, and it looks like James will be gone a few more weeks."

Lucy stares at me from her cat tree.

"Don't look at me in that tone of vision. I know how pathetic I sound. He is just so sweet, and perfect and...you just don't care," I say when Lucy looks away from me. "I think we need a little space because this is getting heated and we don't want to say things we don't mean. I am going to go get an iced coffee. I will see you in a little bit, and I really hope you have calmed down between now and then."

"Meow"

"See, that is what I am talking about. You've got a lot of sass with your frass this morning. Ugh, I will be back shortly."

I fire up my old, run-down car waving at my neighbor and his dog before I pull out onto the road to get a coffee. I might even treat myself to a new lingerie set today. After my argument with Lucy Fur, I deserve a pick-me-up.

I am sitting at the stoplight watching the drive-thru of the coffee joint empty and am thanking my lucky stars that I won't be stuck in a twenty-minute-long line when something slams into my car from behind. I feel my seatbelt dig into my skin along my chest, but before I can register anything else, I turn my head just in time to see a car come from my passenger side and plow into me.

******

"Miss? Miss, can you hear me?"

I swat at the person pulling my eyelids open. "Good gracious! No wonder people talk about a light at the end of the tunnel, it's just you fools playing tricks on us."

The man beside me lets out a low laugh. "I will consider that a yes. Can you tell me your name?"

"Avery. Avery Jones, where am I?" I nervously ask as I try to sit up, but can't.

The mystery man puts a hand on my shoulder from above my line of vision. "Avery, you are in the emergency department. I am Dr. Campbell. Do you remember anything happening today that would have brought you here?"

"Other than the ram from behind and then the Dodge that didn't dodge me, I can only deduce that the wham, slam, thank you ma'am car accident sent me here."

Dr. Campbell steps into my line of sight with a chuckle.

"Wait a dang minute. Am I alive? For real, no jokes. I am alive, right?" I ask, eyes darting around rapidly, the beeping from the heart monitor speeding up.

Dr. Campbell lays a large, warm hand on my shoulder again. "You are very much alive, Avery. For real."

I let out a long sigh. "Good, because for a second there I thought I died and ended up in some TV sitcom version of heaven or something. You know the type of show that has the hot doctor that all the nurses bang in the supply closet and all the patients fall for."

He barks out a laugh. "I will take that as a compliment. Yes, the car accident brought you here. I am about to send you down for some scans to check for internal injuries, and then I will be back to chat with you when we get the result. Is there anyone I can call for you?"

I debate telling him to call James, but decide against it. "No, no one here to call."

He gives a soft nod of his head. "If you think of anyone, just let us know. I will see you shortly, Avery."

I watch the blonde-haired, tanned, hospital Hercules walk out of my room and mull over how bad this day has turned out. I have my call with James tonight, so that will make it better. I will just tell him then.

When I am brought back to the room to wait after my scans, I ask the nurse if she could hand me my phone. She informs me that no phone was brought in with me, only my clothes. *Of course, this is how this day would end.*

Chapter 11
James

Four unanswered calls and seven unanswered emails. I have played back our last conversation we had over and over in my head, and nothing seemed off. No signs that anything was bothering Avery or that she would ghost me.

This plane ride home is torture since I have nothing I can do to take my mind off of this now. At least in North Dakota, I could work out, run, swim, find ways to occupy myself until it was a suitable time to drink myself to sleep, and the weekends that Betty and Lola came to visit helped ease the sting of her ghosting me. Our trip went from a four to six-week trip to an eight-week trip, with the last four weeks being grueling.

"Do you think you could take Betty's Jeep in tomorrow for an oil change? I meant to do it before we left, and it slipped my mind, but it needs to be done before she goes to visit her daughter this weekend." Reed asks, pulling me from my mental spiralling

"Yeah, I can do that first thing in the morning," I offer.

******

Since I don't have an appointment, I have to wait to be squeezed in at the dealership. I don't want time to think, so I decide to walk around the lot and look at vehicles. Jack's graduating in a little over a year, so maybe I will find a graduation gift today. I turn down the next row, where my heart and feet both stop. Avery is walking arm in arm with a tall blonde man, laughing and looking cozy.

I turn around and start to head back to the service department when a young man stops me. "Interested in any of these?"

I shake my head. "No, I am just here for an oil change. If you will excuse me, I must be going."

I walk back into the service department and find a spot where I can watch the sales lot. An older gentleman walks up to Avery and the blonde guy, dangling a set of keys. Avery grabs them from his hand, hugs the older gentleman, and then jumps into the arms of the blonde guy. Watching him spin her around, the joy on her face; I watch the world I was excitedly building crumble in front of me.

***** *

"Gwumpy? Why you updet?" Lola asks as I pour chocolate on her ice cream.

"I am not upset, Princess."

She grabs her spoon and heads to the table. "Yed you awe. I dee it. You be updet fow a while, Gwumpy."

"It is nothing that princesses need to worry about. Come on, let's eat our ice cream before your dad comes in saying it's too late for sweets."

"Well, it is too late for sweets," Reed says, drying his hair from his shower.

107

"Daddy, take a bwite do you don't tawk." Lola says seriously.

Reed and I both laugh and admire this little girl sitting here. Reed makes himself a bowl of ice cream, and we all eat our dessert as Lola tells stories of what happened while we were gone.

"I'll do my check and head back to my place. Goodnight, Princess. Goodnight, Reed," I say when we are done and Lola has started to crash from her sugar high.

My perimeter check is full of anger and sadness. I am angry at myself for allowing Avery into my life, into my bed, into my heart. I was fine before I met her. I felt lonely now and then, but it didn't hurt as bad as this because I didn't know what I was missing. I need a good workout. I will just drive to the gym instead of sitting at home wallowing in my own pity party.

*****

A week after getting home, I am finally coming to terms with the fact that Avery ghosted me. I am about to head to the gym shortly after dinner at the main house, when my phone rings.

"Peter, how can I help you?"

"I know that this is none of my business, but, how do I ask this? Do you need me to call the police on your lady friend? For weeks, she has been coming out here on multiple nights. Most nights, she leaves shortly after you do. Do you need me to manage this?"

I shake my head even though I know he can't see me. "No, I will head over and handle this. I am so sorry, Peter."

"No problem at all, I just didn't know if this was turning into a stalker situation or something. Have a good night, James."

"You too, Peter. Thank you again for everything."

I jump in my car instead of taking the golf cart, I will see what she wants and then head to the gym from there. My mind is racing with all the possibilities of why she would be here. When I pull up to where she always parks, my anger is stroked even more when I see the Jeep she is leaning against. I park and slowly walk around the front of my car.

Avery lifts her head, and I can see sadness written across her face until she locks eyes with me. I see the relieved tears start falling down her cheeks as she opens her arms and runs to me.

"Oh my God. Finally, you are here." She runs over and wraps her arms around my stomach, but I don't hug her back. She looks up into my eyes, and I see her chin start to tremble. "James?"

"Can I help you?" I ask dryly.

Confused, she shakes her head. "What is this, James?"

I remove her arms from around me and step back. "You tell me. You were the one who ghosted me. So, tell me, Avery, what is this?" I ask, pointing to her standing in front of me.

"James, I didn't ghost you," she starts.

I throw my hand up to silence her. "I don't want lies, Avery, there is no need for them here. Save them for your boyfriend who bought you the nice new Jeep. Or is he just another client you break the rules with?"

Avery slaps me across the face and points her finger in my face. "Fuck you, James. You and your head full of assumptions can go straight to hell. I have been coming here five nights a week for a month, waiting for you to come over here and pick me up. You finally do, and this," she exclaims, her hands spread out towards me, "this is how you act. Fuck you." She spins and starts heading for her Jeep.

"Why would I plan to pick you up here after you ignored my calls and emails?" I ask, stomping behind her now.

She whips around. "If you would have just asked instead of making assumptions, you would have learned that my phone was gone, so I had no way of answering you, let alone calling you, and apparently, I didn't back up my phone to my cloud after saving your number. I couldn't get into my email because I am a dumbass and had the password saved to my phone but not my cloud, so I couldn't access it either since I didn't remember the password for my business email."

I cross my arms as she gets into the driver's seat. "So what then? Sorry you aren't responsible enough to keep up with your passwords or your phone?"

She starts her Jeep, her tear-filled, sad eyes find mine. "No, actually it would be, 'sorry you aren't responsible enough to keep up with your passwords, and I am sorry your phone was annihilated in your car wreck that totaled your car.' Semantics, though, right?"

She tries to shut her door, but I stop her. "What car wreck?"

"Let go of my door, James, I am leaving."

"The hell you are, what fucking car wreck, Avery?"

She shakes her head. "Doesn't matter. Now let me go."

She grabs my hand to push it away, but I roll my wrist, grab her arm, and pull her out of the car and into my arms. "What happened, Avery?"

She wipes the tears from her eyes. "Don't worry about it. I'm fine, obviously, so just go back to hating me or whatever and I won't come back. You made it very clear what you think of me tonight, so let's just leave it there." She is trying to pull away from me. "James, just let go. Please."

I fall to my knees in front of her, wrap my arms around her hips and lean my head against her stomach. "Dove, please forget every word I said. Please. I am a jealous asshole. I just got back last Sunday night and saw you the next day at the dealership with that guy. I assumed you ghosted me because you found someone new. Please forgive me. Punish me however you need, but please forgive me."

She runs a hand through my hair. "Get off of your knees."

I look up at her.

She snaps her fingers. "Get the hell up."

I stand in front of her.

"I can't do this anymore tonight," she states, shaking her head. "I get headaches too easily now. Meet me tomorrow at our coffee shop. Ten in the morning. We can talk then."

I grab both of her hands in mine and pull them up to my lips to kiss her knuckles. "I will be there. I am so sorry, Dove."

She pulls her hands from mine and runs her hands through her hair. "Yeah, let's just…we can… yeah. Tomorrow. Just meet me tomorrow."

She jumps back into her Jeep and backs up before taking the circle drive out to the road. I get in my car and do the same so I can head to the gym. Hopefully, Marco is there tonight and is up for boxing. I deserve a good ass kicking right now after what I just said to Avery, and I know Marco will make it hurt.

Chapter 12
Avery

When I pull into the coffee shop parking lot, I see James is already here. I arrived thirty minutes early so that I could find a seat, get my coffee, and mentally prepare for his arrival, but of course, he had to beat me here. Forgiveness points won't be added for his eagerness.

I pull down the mirror and stare at myself, my eyes are a little less puffy than they were an hour ago when I left the house to drive around aimlessly. "Avery," I tell myself in the mirror, "your big girl panties are on. Your ass is looking good, all things considered. You have made it twenty-seven years without needing a man, and you won't start now, Sister. Fix your crown because no one else will. Now go in there, be fair, but take no shit." I smack my ass the best I can and then head inside to face the man who made me cry for the first time in fifteen years.

I make it two steps into the shop when James rises from where he was sitting, pointing to the seat across from him. An iced mocha is already sitting there and waiting for me. As I get closer, I notice bruising on James's face as well as his bottom lip being busted open on one side. I instinctively reach out to touch the bruising under his right eye, but he grabs my wrist to stop me before I can.

"It's nothing," he says, kissing my open palm. "I promise it looks worse than it is."

"Did you get in a fight with your car door after I left last night?"

He shakes his head with a light chuckle. "No, I went to the gym after you left, and my boxing skills aren't quite what they used to be."

"There is a reason most boxers retire before they hit forty. You are past your boxing prime," I state as I sit down.

James runs a hand through his already disheveled hair. "Yeah, lesson learned. Look, Avery, I am sorry. I will never be able to apologize enough for what I said to you last night, and I hate myself for it all. I was jealous, and you were right about me making asinine assumptions. Like I said, I will take any punishment you throw at me, but I want you, I need your forgiveness because I want you in my life."

I look down and start peeling the tag off my coffee cup to keep my hands from reaching out to him. "You hurt me deeply last night, James. I have never offered forgiveness in my life to anyone who has hurt me." He doesn't need to know that a big reason for that is because I don't let anyone close enough to hurt me.

James puts a finger under my chin and lifts my head up to look him in the eyes. "I will bow at your feet, grovel every day of my life if it means that I can be the first on that list."

I bite my bottom lip and stare at him, really stare at him. His eyes have bags under them and purple circles that aren't just bruising. He didn't shave this morning, which is out of character for him. His hair, which is normally effortlessly perfect, is out of place from his hands running through it. He is beating himself up and losing sleep over last night.

I give a light nod. "Okay, we will work towards forgiveness. With that, we start from the beginning. Sundays and Wednesdays are still yours; you have already paid for them, but the rules are firmly in place again. No blurring lines anymore."

He lets out a sigh of relief. "Thank you, Dove. Thank you." He grabs my hands in his. "Now tell me what happened when I was gone."

I tell him about the car wreck and how my car was totaled, the crappy loaner I had for a few weeks before finally getting my insurance money on my old car-which I used as the down payment on my Jeep. I left out the parts about Doctor Calvin Campbell, or Cal. Since I had a concussion from the wreck, I needed someone to stay with me. I had explained to Cal that I had no one here, not a single soul outside of my cat, but she was mad at me that day, which is why I left the house to begin with.

Though it was unethical, he felt bad for me and waited to release me until his shift was about to end. He drove me home and stayed with me that first night to watch over me. Him on my chair and me on my couch, we spent the entire night talking about his work and mine. He told me how he would hire me since he doesn't have time for dating, but misses human contact outside of the hospital.

He went with me to get my Jeep because it was his uncle who worked out the financing for me and helped me get what I needed from my bank since I don't have a traditional job. James doesn't need to know all of that, nor can I tell him now that Cal is a client of mine.

After James tells me of his time in North Dakota with the ass pinching hotel owner, he slides a bag across the table to me. "I got this for you while I was up there. I saw it and it made me think of you."

"Thank you," I open the bag and find a small stuffed turtle. My smile is genuine when I look up at James. "He is the cutest gift I have ever received."

"When I saw him, I instantly thought of us. So, Ring Mistress, what will his name be?"

"Shelldon," I say confidently. "My wise friend Shelldon."

"Shelldon it is," he laughs out.

"I am glad you came to talk with me, and I have enjoyed our talk but, I have to get going."

"Oh, of course. Big movie plans with Lucy Fur?" he asks.

I shake my head while tucking Shelldon into my purse. "No, I have work tonight."

His face drops. "Of course. I am sorry. Yeah, let's ugh… let's get you out of here. Do you want another coffee for the road?"

"No, I am good. Thank you, though."

"Okay, I will walk you out."

We walk outside to my Jeep. "I really am glad we talked," I tell James.

"Me too. Can I hug you, or would that be considered blurring the lines?"

I blow out a puff of air. "I can allow a hug."

His arms wrap around me, and I find myself relaxing being in his arms again. His warmth and smell instantly make me feel more at ease. I missed this. I missed him. I need to pull myself back and remember last night. I can work to forgive him, but forgetting is not an option.

"I will see you Wednesday. Same time, same place?" I ask as I pull myself out of his arms.

A small smile spreads across his lips. "Yeah, same time and place. See you then, Avery."

******

I am walking up to Cal's door. It's been eight hours since I left the coffee shop, but I don't feel any better about how we left things. I want to be at James's house right now. I want to be curled up with him, watching and singing along to some musical. I want his arms around me and his lips on me. I want to rewind time and make our driveway dispute to never have happened. Instead, I am standing here on the porch of a man who has been so sweet and good to me, but I feel nothing more than friendship for.

"Avery, I thought I heard you pull up. How are you liking the new vehicle?" Cal asks before kissing both of my cheeks.

"I love it, I'm already looking at some rose gold door handles that I think I want to get. She needs some femininity. Rosalind needs a little adornment," I say, stepping into Cal's beach bungalow.

"I imagine she will look just as stunning as her owner when you do. Want anything before we start?" he asks.

I shake my head. "Nope, let's start this game of rummy so I can whoop your ass."

Like every night with Cal, we start off with a card or board game where we catch up on life since we last saw each other. I tell him about Lucy, and he tells me stories about work, and how his emergency department shifts are easing up now that the hospital is fully staffed.

After following through with whooping his ass in cards, we head to his room where I will cuddle him for an hour before heading home for the night.

"Avery, Honey, are you okay? You seem a little distant tonight," he says, rubbing my arm that is draped over him.

I didn't realize I sucked that badly at hiding my emotions. "Yeah, just girly stuff, you know how we are around shark week," I lie.

He hums. "Gotcha, need me to get some chocolate for tomorrow?"

I give his arm a squeeze. "You are the best, but no thank you. I should be feeling better by tomorrow. Now quit worrying about me, this is your time."

I lay my head against his back, hoping to hide my lies and emotions. I have never counted down the time with a client, but tonight I am. I want to go home and release all these built-up emotions that have taken over me today. I don't know if I need to cry, sing it out, have an orgasm or what, but I need to figure something out to help me get over this before Wednesday.

******

Tuesday wasn't quite as bad. I still was not fully present with Cal, and I feel awful for that, but I was able to hide it better at least.

When I woke up this morning, I decided I needed a pick-me-up before seeing James tonight. I went out for a coffee, pedicure, and then I hit the mall to find the most modest but cute, comfy outfit I could find. I opted for a pair of pants with a short-sleeve shirt lounge set. I need all the protection and armor I can have tonight. By the time I pull into Peter's driveway, I feel like I am prepared to handle tonight professionally.

I was wrong. So horribly wrong.

Chapter 13
James

I pull up to find Avery giving herself a little pep talk in her visor mirror. I sit there and watch her, knowing I am the reason she feels she has to pep herself up just to see me, just like at the coffee shop. I watched her build herself up to even open the Jeep door, and it gutted me just as much then as it does now. If I were a good man, I would tell her that she has no obligation to me. Like I told her in the beginning, if we part ways, the money is still hers no matter what. But I am a selfish man when it comes to Avery. A very selfish man.

"Good evening," I say when she finally gets out of her Jeep and heads over to the golf cart.

"Good evening to you, too," she states with a fake smile plastered on her face.

"None of that, Dove, none of that."

She whips her head to face me. "None of what?"

I point to her face. "None of that fake stuff. I'd rather you curse me than be fake around me."

She shrugs. "Fine then. Come on, asshole, take me to your humble abode so I can shell you."

I glance over and see a real grin on her face now. "Much better."

I already pulled up a musical for us to watch before going to pick her up. I put the flowers in the living room this time instead of the bedroom. A bottle of water is out on the side table with orange slices in Tupperware next to it.

"I will go change really quickly. Meet you out here in a minute," she says as she heads to my bedroom.

I glance around one last time to make sure everything looks okay, run to the laundry room and throw on the sweatpants I had folded in there and a t-shirt just to make sure she is comfortable tonight. I will not push her away by trying to rush her. I make my glass of milk, and when I get to the couch, I see that she is already sitting there, head down, looking at her clasped hands.

"Avery?"

She looks up, and I watch her mask fall into place. "Alright, Turtle, assume the position."

I just nod my head, lay down in my spot on the couch, and wait for her to get settled behind me. I don't miss the fact that she is not wearing her old ensembles tonight; tonight, it is an outfit that covers nearly her whole body. "Hope this movie is okay. I don't recall us ever talking about whether it was a favorite or not, but I figured you would like it."

She shrugs behind me. "Yeah, it's a good one."

I press play and soak in her distant cuddles. There is no mending feeling radiating from her like there usually is, not for me at least. There is also no singing along throughout this movie. Maybe I am hurting her by being selfish and making her come here.

The credits start rolling, and Avery stands. "Such a good one. I am going to head back to my Jeep now. I will see you on Sunday. Same time, same place."

I jump up. "Oh, give me a second, I will drive you over there."

She shakes her head. "No, really, I will walk. I could use the fresh air."

"Avery, it's nearly a mile just to get to the gate and then nearly half a mile to Peter's driveway. It is dark out, let me drive you."

Avery puts her hand on my chest. "James, I want to walk. Thank you, though."

I nod. "Okay, I will watch the cameras and hit the button to open the gate when you get close to it. Let me put my number back in your phone in case you change your mind along the way. I will come grab you and take you the rest of the way."

She hands me her phone, I add my information quickly, hand it back to her, and then walk her to the front door.

"Thank you for coming tonight. See you Sunday," I say before leaning down to kiss the top of her head.

She turns her head slightly to avoid my kiss and pats my chest. "See you Sunday."

I shut the door behind me and pace the living room for a second before going to my small office to look at the cameras and hit the button when I need to. When she has made it past the gate and I can no longer watch her, I head to my bedroom. I feel my heart crack when I see my sweatshirt sitting on my bed, folded neatly on the corner.

******

The next six weeks followed the same pattern. I would pick Avery up, she would stay long enough for a movie, and then she would walk back to her Jeep. She would only cuddle me from behind me and would never rake her hands over my arms or anything. She really did feel like a shell now, hollow and heavy. Every visit, she would start to talk a little more. A joke here or there, a sly remark about the movie we were watching, but still no singing. When she came over on the seventh week, I was finally prepared to end her suffering. I was ready to tell her that she didn't have to come by anymore, that I was done dulling her sparkle, but then she surprised me.

"Can I pick the movie tonight?" she asks as we walk into my house.

"Anything you want," I say as I close the door behind us.

"Sweet. Okay, meet you out here in a few."

I walk over to the laundry room to grab my sweats and t-shirt, throw them on real fast, check this week's flower arrangement for the hundredth time and then sit on the couch. I look up to see Avery walking back into the living room in her old outfit, the first one she wore over here nearly five months ago. I turn my eyes to the TV quickly to avoid making her feel uncomfortable.

"Here ya go." I pass her the remote.

"Thanks. Now assume the position."

She gets behind me while the opening credits for her movie start up, within minutes, she is softly singing along behind me. Not in her old Avery way- this one is guarded- but she is singing. I relax under her more than I have in months, and I feel her do the same.

After the movie is over and she gets prepared to leave, it is a little less sad tonight.

"Well, glad to see your ears aren't bleeding after that," she says, turning my face side to side.

"When you said you wanted to pick the movie tonight, I shoved some cotton down deep in there just in case," I say jokingly.

Avery playfully smacks my arm. "You are so funny. Shithead. I will see you Wednesday."

"See you Wednesday," I respond, putting my hands in my pockets to stop myself from reaching out to hug her.

She reaches out and pats my arm. "Goodnight, James."

"Goodnight, Avery."

I watch her walk for a bit from the open door, and just before I was about to turn around and head inside, she turned back and gave me a smile. For the first time in a long while, I had renewed faith that I would get my dove back. That maybe I didn't screw everything up completely. Her birthday is in three weeks. I should start planning a surprise now.

Chapter 14
Avery

Avery,

I wish I could make it out to celebrate our birthdays together, but things are just crazy here. Tim's work schedule has been rough. He is working late most evenings and having to go on a lot of business trips lately. He promised to take me to these cute little cabins that aren't too far away for my birthday, since he has been working so much. After the new year, I will try to pinpoint a week that would work for me to fly out.

Money is tight right now. Memaw says hi and happy birthday. She asked if you want her to send you some of her cookies for your birthday. Well, I told her to let me ask you before she just sends them. I have to make this one short, but I will send another letter later. I have to tell you about what happened at work the other day. For now, I will just say that what happened in Final Destination shouldn't be possible, but totally could be if you try to use a stool to block the door rather than just use the lock that is on it. It was crazy! Talk soon. I love you!

Sandy

"Well, Lucy, looks like it will just be us for my birthday this year. Maybe Keri from the coffee shop would want to get together and do something."

"Meow."

"Well, no. We haven't talked outside of the coffee shop, but it wouldn't hurt to ask. We have talked a lot over the last couple of months since she waits for me to show up to take her breaks. That has to count for something. I will ask her when I go in tomorrow."

"Meooooow."

"If you don't have anything nice to say, Lucy, just don't say anything at all."

******

It has been a few weeks since things started to feel normal with James again. We both have fallen back into friendly banter, and I am annoying him with my singing again. I still have times where I want to take things fully back to how it was before our fight, but I know that I need just a little more time before we get there. When he pulls up beside me on the golf cart tonight, I am genuinely happy to see his smile.

"You look awfully chipper tonight," I say.

"I am. I have a surprise for you, and I suck at hiding my excitement when it comes to surprises."

"Now I am nervous."

He lets out a soft laugh. "Don't be."

The rest of the ride to his house is comfortable silence. When we get to his house, he hands me a sleep mask to cover my eyes with.

"Really?" I ask, holding it out on one finger.

"Really. Humor me, just for a minute."

"Fine." I succumb.

James puts his large hands on my shoulders; this is the first time he has touched me since my first night coming back here. I forgot how big his hands are. Maybe it's the chill from the winter wind or from me not wearing adequate jackets in winter, but they are sending a much-needed warmth through me, too.

"Okay, stand here. Yeah," he says once he has me positioned where he wants me. "Now count to thirty and then remove the blindfold."

I feel his hands leave my shoulders and hear him shuffle across the room. When I get to thirty, I remove the mask and take in my surroundings.

A banner is hanging from the ceiling that reads, "Happy Birthday Avery!" Flowers and candles fill the room, and James is standing in front of the counter with a party hat on his head with the biggest smile I have ever seen spread across his face.

"Since I won't see you Saturday, I figured we would have an early birthday party, complete with noise makers that are more annoying than your singing," he jokes.

Tears fill my eyes. "This is fabulous, James."

"Oh crap, I forgot something. Turn around and don't peek."

I let out a breathy laugh, but I do as he says.

"Okay, turn back around."

I turn around and fall to my knees when I see that he is standing in front of me holding a cupcake with a candle coming out of it in his hand. A cupcake with white buttercream frosting, pink sprinkles, and a pink wrapper around it. A cupcake identical to the cupcake Colin gave me fifteen years ago.

I grab my chest. "What? What the actual fuck? No, no." I stand up and turn for the door, but collapse before I do.

*****

"What did I tell you last time about shining that damned light in my eyes, Cal," I mumble.

"Miss Avery, my name is Peter. I live next door, where you park. You fainted, dear. Does anything hurt?"

"Please tell me you are kidding," I turn my head to see an older gentleman with a bag open beside him. Behind him, I see James pacing nervously. "You aren't kidding."

Peter shakes his head while wearing a friendly smile. "No, dear, I am not kidding. Do you have a history of fainting? Any diagnosis that would have caused you to faint?"

I put my hand on my chest. "No, it was just a panic attack. I will be okay."

"Are you seeing someone?" he asks.

I nod as I pull myself up to sit. "Yeah, I have been seeing her for years. I am so sorry."

"Don't apologize, dear, relax for a bit. James said you hit your head when you fell, so you need to have someone stay with you tonight to watch for signs of a concussion. James, if you need anything else, just call me, but I think she will be okay," Peter says as he winks my way.

"You two have a good night, and happy early birthday, dear."

"Thank you."

I shift around to stand, and James runs over to help me. He grabs under my elbow and helps me to my feet. I feel a little dizzy still and don't fight him when he picks me up bridal style and carries me over to his couch.

"Lay here, I am going to get you a water with an orange slice."

When he comes back over to me, he hands me the drink and then sits on the floor next to the couch. "What happened?"

"I had a panic attack, nothing to worry about."

He scoffs. "I know that. I meant, what happened to cause you to have panic attacks?"

"Oh, James, that's not party talk," I try to joke, but it comes out sounding weak.

"If you don't want to talk about it, that's fine, but what did I do to trigger it? You were fine one second, and then I showed you the cupcake, and you freaked out."

I place a hand on his arm. "Can you throw the cupcake away?"

He looks at me, puzzled. "The cupcake? Yeah, I will throw it away right now."

He jumps up from the floor, and I hear him opening the lid to the trash can before hearing a light thud from the cupcake hitting the bottom.

"So, now that this birthday party has turned into an impromptu sleepover, what does the birthday girl want to do first?" James asks as he walks back over to me.

"Nails, face masks, and prank call the neighbors. We will skip Peter since we have already included him tonight," I say with my hands clapping in front of me.

"Well, I am glad I was prepared for such a night," he says, walking up behind me and placing a gift bag on my stomach.

Inside, I find a few different nail polish options, face masks, headbands, foot and hand moisturizing gloves, a few gift cards for local boutiques, and a gift certificate for a one-hour massage at a local salon.

My first movie pick was a hilarious musical with my Queen Celine's music being the center of it. I didn't hold back my singing at all. James even joined in on a few songs.

"James, this is the best birthday I could have asked for- possible concussion and all. The only thing that would have made today perfect was if Sandy were here to join us," I say as I am bent over his foot, painting his toenails purple.

"I am glad I could salvage the night and make it memorable. Tell me about Sandy," he states, bent over my foot and painting my toenails pink.

*****

After nails, face masks, and movie karaoke, we settled on the couch for a Christmas movie. I woke up in the middle of the night with our legs intertwined, and the couch throw blanket over my body. There is nowhere else I would want to be right now. I take in James' sleeping face for another moment before turning my head and going back to sleep.

Chapter 15
James

The sun shining in my eyes wakes me up. I am always up before the sun rises, so I already know I overslept. I feel the weight of Avery on my legs and look down to see her peacefully sleeping still. She never explained how a cupcake had caused a panic attack, but I would be lying if I said I didn't like the fact that it caused her to stay the night here. Even if it was just for safety concerns, for the first time in months, Avery didn't walk out of my house after a movie. She didn't leave me here to remember all I had done wrong. I got my 'one more' night that I had been hoping for. I don't want to wake her, but I need to find my phone to text Reed to let him know that I will be preoccupied today.

I roll as smoothly as I can off the couch but am unsuccessful in my task at hand. "Good morning, how are you feeling?"

Avery throws her arm over her eyes. "Like a vampire, I am assuming. Why is it so bright in here?"

I can't suppress my grin. "Because some really hot dumbass decided against curtains or blinds."

"Subjective," she utters, rolling into the back of the couch.

"Subjective?" I guffaw. "You think me being hot is subjective?"

"James, sweet cheeks, have you not learned that you are truly the worst with assumptions? Dumbass was the subjective word. I would have gone with 'hot, decoratively challenged man decided against curtains or blinds.' But if you prefer dumbass, it is your story; write it your way." She pulls her head from against the couch to look at me with a shit eating grin.

"If you weren't so fragile right now, I would pull you over my knee and spank you for being such a brat." I stand and kiss the top of her head. "But it just so happens that you are. What do you want me to make you for breakfast?"

She sits up quickly. "Nothing. I need to head home. Lucy Fur will be furious with me as it is, no need to add to it."

"Sorry, Dove, you aren't allowed to drive for twenty-four hours. You have about fourteen more hours to go. How about I drive you home? I will spend the next fourteen hours catering to your every whim, and then I will get someone to bring me back here."

"Let's meet in the middle. You drive me home, cater to me for ten hours and then I bring you back because I have to work tonight," she counteroffers.

"You should probably take tonight off, just to be safe," I say as I pull down the coffee and filters from the cabinet.

"I can't. Not on Thursdays and Fridays. It isn't possible," she says with a shake of her head.

"Avery, your health should be more important than a client. Always."

"Not this one. He isn't like you; his situation calls for a companion when his daughter can't be home. She has to work tonight, so I have to work tonight."

I nod, realizing the importance of what she is saying without her speaking the words. "Okay. I understand. I will agree to your counteroffer, but add a small amendment to our agreement: I want you to call me when you make it home tonight after work. Just so I know that you made it home safely."

"So bossy, but deal," she says as she moves around to start throwing her things into her bag.

I smile over my shoulder at her and abandon my coffee prep. "Coffee joint on the way?"

She smiles now. "Yeah, and then I will make you the best breakfast burrito bowl you have ever had in your life."

******

"Betty, I have four days left to find her a Christmas gift, and I can't think of anything that is good enough for her. She loved the birthday gifts she got a couple of weeks ago. I don't want to repeat any of those, and I already got a stack of gift cards for her stocking. Help me, please?" I ask her while she rummages around the kitchen for the ingredients she is looking for.

"Jamesy Dear, you have been seeing this woman for six months now. What have you noticed that she loves?"

I shrug. "She loves singing, musicals, extremely soft pajamas, her best friend Sandy back in Texas, her cat Lucy, and sleeping."

Betty lets out a motherly laugh. "And out of all of those, which can you figure out a special gift from?"

I kiss Betty's wrinkled cheek. "You are brilliant! Thank you for always knowing the answer to everything."

"Yeah, yeah, yeah. Now, about my Christmas gift: I love you boys, our princess, my children, Luke Evans, Sam Heughan, and unicorns. I already have access to three things on my list; I am not equipped the way one of them prefers, and unicorns would be awfully hard to find. So, I will take my Sam Heughan in a size, yes please, under the tree. You don't have much time, my boy. Better get on it to get your shopping list taken care of," she says, shooing me out of her kitchen.

"Betty, you naughty, naughty woman. Sam wouldn't know what to do with you," I jest.

"You obviously didn't watch him and Claire because I bet he sure would," she says with a shimmy. "Now go and don't come back until I holler that dinner is ready."

"Yes, ma'am. If you need me, you know where I will be."

******

I have ten minutes before I need to head over to Peter's driveway. I check the fresh flowers in the living room, adjust the out-of-place string lights on the tree I had Lola help me put up and decorate this morning, set out the ingredients to make hot chocolate and queue up a Christmas classic. Grabbing my coat, I walk over to the front door and open it to nearly have a heart attack.

"Merry Christmas!" Avery yells, holding a gift out in front of her.

"Good Lord, Woman, you nearly gave me a heart attack. Get in here." I wrap my hand around her wrist and pull her into me. "Merry Christmas," I say with a kiss to the top of her head.

"Hurry, open it. I have nearly died holding this secret in! Hurry," she says, bouncing foot to foot.

I take the thin, rectangular box from her and head to the couch. "Hold your horses. Sit down and let me get yours."

"James! This tree! It is gorgeous!" She is standing still in front of the seven-foot tree decorated with white lights, different shades and sizes of pink and white ornaments that sparkle with the lights, and a brunette angel sitting atop it.

"Thank you, I assumed you would like it."

She turns to face me. "Finally, you make one good assumption. Took you long enough." She turns to face the tree again, hand pulled up to her mouth. "Did you do this for me?"

"Of course I did. Now get over here so we can open our presents and watch our Christmas movie."

She walks over and sits next to me; I hand her the stocking I made for her. I sit there admiring her while she goes through the gift cards, excitement written all over her face, until she opens her big gift, and her face falls.

"You always talk about how much you miss Sandy; I wanted to get you something I knew you could use. The flight dates are open, so you can decide when to go. Just let me know and I will set it up. First class, both ways."

Tears are falling from her beautiful eyes. "Thank you, James, I have been wanting to go back to see her but just haven't been able to convince myself to."

I lean over and wipe her tears away. "You say that like you don't want to go there. I can change the destination if you want to go somewhere else."

She grabs my wrist. "No, I need to go back there. Thank you. This truly was such a thoughtful gift."

I kiss her wrist and then open my gift.

"Isn't it beautiful?" she asks.

I nod. "It is."

"The artist is local. She has an intriguing story: After a routine hospital procedure took two of her fingers and changed her life, she found this form of art during physical therapy. If the painting wasn't already beautiful on its own, her strength and story make it stunning," Avery explains excitedly.

"Let's go hang it in my bedroom," I say.

"Your bedroom?" she asks.

"Yeah, where else would I put this painting? The turtle is us. I want it to be the last thing I see at night and the first thing I see in the morning."

Avery blushes. "You really love it?"

"Of course I do, it reminds me of you."

Avery lunges forward, wrapping her arms around my neck. "You are too good sometimes."

I wrap an arm around her waist. "Remember that the next time I make you mad." I stand, lifting her with me.

"Now come on, we have to find Shelly here a place to hang."

Chapter 16
Avery

Avery,

I hope your birthday and Christmas were better than mine. Tim ended up working both, so we didn't make it to the cabins. At least I had Memaw and Uncle Alex to spend both of them with. Tim swore he would make it at some point on Christmas Day, but never did. Memaw even made his favorite meal rather than our traditional Christmas dinner. I am pretty disappointed about it all, but I just need to get over it. I will get over it, just not yet.

I had a walk down memory lane today! Do you remember that heifer Heather? The one that always made fun of my bucked teeth and called you a slut on the first day of eighth grade? Well, I was at the grocery store, and she approached me. She tried to get me to join her in selling some overpriced products. Like she didn't make half of my life hell? I can't stand a mean girl who hides behind a fake smile.

In case you are wondering, her husband ended up having an affair with the nanny, she has hemorrhoids that she hasn't been able to get rid of since giving birth three years ago, and she showed me how her hairpiece is nearly impossible to see.

Enough about my fun, small-town adventures. Everything going alright on the East Coast? I haven't heard from you in a couple of weeks. I miss you and I love you!

Sandy

Sandy,

I have made three friends this month, so I have actually been away from my house a lot more. Keri, who works at the coffee shop down the road I told you about, and her cousins, Tasha and Talia. We have spent every Saturday out barhopping now that the twins are twenty-one. They make me feel young again...or maybe for the first time. I don't know. I am seven years late for the drinking and partying craze, but I am really enjoying it. I feel like carefree me from before.

My birthday was fun! I went out dancing. One of my customers got me the best birthday gift ever! A round-trip flight to come and see you!!! I am thinking I will fly out in late April so we can go to that music festival in Stephenville that you always want to go to, but never do. Or maybe I will wait until the 4th of July so we can go to the lake we always went to as kids. My cousin out in Dallas has a boat that she and her husband could take us out on for the day. Let me know which one works for your schedule, and we will get it planned. Happy New Year, Peach! I love you and miss you, too!

Your favorite!

******

"Lucy, since Cal was called into work, you know what that means for tonight!"

Cal was not overly thrilled about work tonight. He swears that New Year's Eve, 4th of July, Halloween, Thanksgiving, and any full moon will take two years off your life for each shift of these that you work. He has had to work them all since I met him.

I head to my room and pull out my 'rich widow robe' that Cal got me for Christmas, and put it over the silk nighty he got me for my birthday. Both a beautiful, deep, purple.

I pull my hair up into an old Hollywood-inspired sideswept wave, grab my phone and snap a few pictures to send to Sandy in my next email to her. Her memaw used to spend every New Year's Eve in a similar ensemble watching old Hitchcock films to ring in the new year, which became one of mine and Sandy's favorite traditions. Two little girls running around the house with sheets held together by safety pins to look like fancy robes, plastic flutes filled with sparkling grape juice, and old black and white films. We thought we were the classiest girls to ever walk the ground of our hometown. Every year, I have repeated this tradition, but this is my first year to have an actual robe and not just poking holes in my sheets.

I walk to the kitchen and pour my sparkling grape juice into a champagne flute, grab my veggie tray, and head to my couch. I am halfway through Rebecca when I hear a knock at my door. Before opening, I grab my sock-covered bat and hold it beside me so it is hidden when I crack the door open.

"It's okay, honey, I will check to see who it is, just keep that vicious dog with you in the other room while I do," I yell loudly. Hopefully, whoever is on the other side of the door will think I am not vulnerable and alone and that if they try something, a massive dog will tear their face off.

I open the door to a beautiful man smiling at me.

"Please, please keep the vicious dog in the other room, honey," James mockingly whines.

I smack his chest. "Shut up, loser. What are you doing here?"

James looks at his watch. "I was hoping you were home, and I have three minutes until I need the kiss that will bring me good luck for the new year." He opens his arms to me. "So here I am, and here you are looking gorgeous." He doesn't even try to hide the way his eyes rake over every inch of my body.

I can't stop the smile that takes over my face. "You are just too much some days and just enough on others. Come on." I open the door wider, and he notices my bat.

"Did your bat get cold?" he asks, pointing to my wooden bat sporting a rainbow-colored toe sock from the early 2000s.

I wave it around in the air. "No, Einstein. I am going to pretend to hit you, and you grab the bat from me."

I swing it towards him slowly, he grabs the body of the bat closest to him, and the sock slides off. He looks down at his hand, and while he does, I use this split second to throw a light tap to his ass with the bat.

"See, functionally adorned. You can't take the bat with my first swing, which gives me a chance for a second one that will actually hit ya."

James grabs my waist and pulls me into him. "You are the smartest woman I know."

I look up into his eyes. "Didn't we have this talk before about flattery?"

"We did, and I told you that I don't lie." The way he is staring into my eyes, I swear he can read my thoughts. He glances at his watch. " 8.7.6.5.4."

I can feel a burning need in my core.

"3.2."

I throw my arms around his neck and jump up; he catches me under my thighs. My legs wrap around him, and our mouths collide. Desperate, deep, needy. This kiss is relaying the months of missing each other in this way. His arms tighten around me, and we bump around the living room until we fall onto my couch.

My robe falls open, and my silk nightgown rides high up on my thighs, exposing the matching thong underneath. James's hands roam over my exposed skin, leaving goosebumps in it's trail.

"God, I missed you," James says after pulling away and laying his forehead on my chest.

"It hasn't even been forty-eight hours since I left your house," I say to him.

"I wasn't talking to *you*. I was talking to you," he kisses my mouth. "And you." He kisses my chest over my heart, that is racing frantically. "And you," he says, kissing the outside of one of my thighs before coming back up to kiss me on the mouth.

Even though I want to continue kissing him and seeing where this will lead, the smart part of my brain is screaming at me to tap the brakes. I run my fingers through his hair. "Shut up and lie down, you are interrupting one of my favorites," I say with a grin.

James lays his head on my chest, body draped over mine, and snakes his arms around my waist. "Yes, ma'am."

By the end of the movie, I can feel his deep breathing crushing me. "James, you are squishing me. Wake up," I say, patting his back with just enough force to startle him.

"My Dove," he whispers groggily, "just one more night, please." His eyes still closed, he drops back onto my stomach.

"James, wake up, come on, you can stay, but my couch isn't where I am sleeping tonight." I wiggle, trying to get out from under him.

He lifts his weight off of me, opens his eyes and takes in his surroundings. "I am sorry, I will go," he says as he wipes his eyes and lightly smacks his cheek to wake himself up.

"You just said you want one more night, do you not want one more night?" I ask.

"I will always want one more night with you. Always."

I stand and grab his hand. "Then get your ass up, my couch isn't as big as yours. Let's go to bed."

I fall asleep wrapped in his arms, feeling safer and more content than I have in a long while. I have never had a man in my bed. Ever. But he makes it feel like he belongs here with me.

******

"Beth, how was work tonight?" I ask her when she walks in the door, looking exhausted.

"Full of sleazy men that are cheating on their wives and sleazy men that can't respect anyone long enough to obtain a wife. And they were cheap too," she moans as she looks up at the ceiling. "I danced so much that by one, I gave up and just stood there swaying."

I bark out a laugh. "I am sorry, sugar. I have something for you: Happy Valentine's Day!" I hand her the gift certificate I picked up for her this morning. "The second half of this gift is a free night of yours truly warming the seat next to your dad for free ninety-nine. You need a night to recharge your battery or drain them if ya know what I mean. Either way, you pick the night and I am here."

"You are the greatest thing that ever fell into my life, you know that?" she asks as she pulls me in for a hug.

"I know. I am going to head out. Your dad had a really good night, by the way. He was calm and kept telling me stories about your mom and all of their Valentine's Days together. Your dad sure did love your mom."

Beth nods with a wide grin on her face now. "He did, he showed her every day. That is why I am still single; no man could beat the example he set for how a husband should treat a wife."

"I'm jealous. Good night, Beth, see you next week unless you need me sooner." I leave with a wink.

Her words about her father echos in my mind as I drive home. I know my dad loves my mom, he tells her all the time. But I can't remember a time that I could see it or feel it. Almost like they are just with each other because it's convenient. The best example I have is from movies, and those just aren't quite as dependable. I am lost in my own thoughts until I pull into my driveway and see James's car parked in my spot.

I step out of my Jeep and try to hide my smile when I walk up my sidewalk to find him sitting on my swing, flowers and a small bag in hand.

"Well, my, my Sir, you keep showing up around these parts of town and I may begin to think you are smitten with me." I fan myself with my hand.

He eyes me up and down. "Who wouldn't be when you are walking around in sweats like that? I should lock you away so other men can't see how sexy you are." He grabs my hip and pulls me against his chest, running his hand up my back. "Is that an old cotton sports bra under that baggy shirt, too? Damn, Dove, you are driving me wild," he growls before nipping my ear.

I cackle- literally cackle- at his words. "Play your cards right and I will even pull my hair up in a lopsided bun, just for you."

"You know just what to say to rev my engine, woman. Now, unlock your door and let's get you inside before all the men in this town start migrating to your yard to try to steal you from me."

I lean up on my tip toes and kiss his cheek. "As if they even could." I turn around, unlock my front door, and pull him in by his shirt.

"Wait here for me," I say as I skip off to my room.

I tug off my sweats, hideous shirt, and bra. Digging around in my drawer, I find the outfit I bought just for tonight in case he showed up like he has been most nights. It is a simple red silky camisole and shorts set. I grab the gift I bought for him and head back to my living room. James is sitting on my couch with Lucy on his lap, his fingers lazily stroking her while she kneads into his leg.

I slowly step out of the hallway towards the kitchen. "Need a drink or anything?"

James stares at me wide-eyed. "I'll have whatever you are having."

"I'm having rum, so if you are having the same, get comfy." I bend over to grab the rum from the bottom shelf on the door of the fridge. I peek around me to see James slack-jawed and hypnotized by the view I am giving him. Without standing, I ask, "Orange juice, cranberry juice, or both?" I wiggle my ass like I am shuffling around looking for everything.

"Whatever you want, Dove."

I peek another glance at him and see he is gripping the couch cushion so hard that I may need to throw a blanket on it to hide the marks he is most likely leaving behind. "Both it is." I begin making our drinks before sauntering over to the couch.

"You could have stayed in your sweats if you were more comfortable," he says weakly.

"I am comfortable. Happy Valentine's Day," I say softly, handing him his gift.

He opens the bag and barks out a deep laugh. "Pray tell, Dove, where and when do you want me to wear this?" He unfolds the mankini with the crotch of an elephant's trunk.

I shrug. "That is entirely up to you. When I saw it, I thought of you."

He laughs again. "One day, I will catch you by surprise wearing only this."

"I can't wait," I say with a smile.

"Now, your turn." He hands me a small bag.

I pull out a small box and open it to find a beautiful necklace with a small turtle pendant, the shell is a small ruby. I gasp, "James, this is absolutely beautiful!"

"Come here, let's put it on you."

I turn my back to him, and he lays the necklace over my chest, his knuckles sliding over my skin, making me shiver. I feel like my skin is vibrating from his light touch.

"There we go. Turn around, let me see it."

I turn around and his fingers loop under the necklace on either side to help shift it into place. Slowly, his knuckles slide down my chest to end just under the top of my cami between my breasts. My eyes are locked on his fingers, my breath uneven. I can tell my nipples are as hard as diamonds, and since I took my bra off, the slightest movement of the silk is making me ache for more. His finger slides up my chest and neck before hooking under my chin and lifting my head up so that I am staring into his eyes that mirror mine: half lidded and full of lust.

"Kiss me," I whisper.

"Yes, ma'am," he groans as he leans forward and places the gentlest kiss on my slightly parted lips.

I growl, "James."

"You are the one running the show, Dove," he says kissing me softly again.

"Take me to bed," I gasp out

"Safe word?"

"Mahout."

James pulls me onto his lap with one arm behind my back and one under my ass as he stands and moves us to my bedroom. He puts me on my bed and stands between my legs while he pulls his shirt up over his head. I watch as the muscles in his stomach flex with each move he makes and reach out to feel them under my touch. I watch in amazement as my touch sends a shiver down his body.

I sit up, looking him in the eyes as I unbutton his jeans and pull them down his thick and muscular thighs. I drop my gaze to take in how beautiful this man looks in front of me before looking back at his face and pulling his boxer briefs down. "I want you tonight. All of you."

James leans forward to start kissing me. I crawl towards the top of the bed as he moves in sync above me.

"I want to watch you play with yourself," I say breathlessly. "I want you to show me what you like."

James leans back and kneels in front of me, one hand held in front of my mouth. "Lick it."

I flatten my tongue and lick up his hand. He grabs his shaft with that hand and starts slowly stroking himself. I take this time to grab my top and lift it over my head before removing my shorts, leaving myself bare before him. With no shame at all, his eyes move from my chest down to my bare pussy.

"Show me what you like, Dove. Show me how you touch yourself when you are alone."

I lean back against the pillows and spread myself wide before him. I pull two fingers into my mouth before pulling them out and dropping them to my pussy. I slide my fingers down to spread my lips for him to see how wet I am from him. For him. I slide two fingers inside me with one hand and use my other hand to pinch my clit between two fingers.

"Fuck, Dove. Add another finger. Get yourself ready for me," he growls.

I add a third finger and moan from how stretched I already feel. "James, please, I need you."

James leans over me and then stops abruptly. "Shit. I did not expect any of this to happen tonight. Do you have a condom?"

"I am a virgin, James. I don't keep condoms lying around for funsies."

"Okay, well then I will just make you feel good tonight," he says as he leans down to kiss me.

I bite his lip. "I am a virgin, I am clean, and I got on birth control the week of your birthday. If you are okay with no condom, I am."

"Are you serious right now?" he asks, not able to hide his surprise.

"Yeah, unless it grosses you out or something. I mean, you are clean, right?" I ask.

"I'm clean and why would I be grossed out? I meant are you serious about when you got on birth control?"

"Yeah."

"You are something. Now shut up so I can take care of you," he says as he smiles against my lips. "If it hurts, tell me and we'll stop."

I nod. "Okay."

James gives me one last look in my eyes before coming in to kiss me again. The head of his cock slides up from my slit to my clit, spreading my arousal around before notching his head against my opening. Slowly, he starts thrusting into me, a little at a time. When he meets resistance, he stills and looks me in the eyes, whispering, "This is going to burn and feel uncomfortable for about a minute. You say the word, and we stop. Once I am fully in, I am going to wait until I feel you loosen around me. Okay?"

"Okay," I whisper.

"Kiss me, Dove."

I do as he says and I kiss him. With my arms around his neck, pulling him close to me as I kiss him through the pain. When he starts his thrusting again, the pain is gone and replaced with pure pleasure.

He leans back. "Look at you, Dove. Look at your perfect pussy wrapped around me."

I lean forward to look and immediately throw my head back, arching my back from how that made him feel inside me. My breaths are erratic, I can't control my moaning, and I can feel an orgasm building inside me with every pump of him.

"You are so damn magnificent," he mutters. His breath matches mine and his thumb finds my clit.

I am bucking my hips to meet his, his thumb driving me wild. "James, I'm going to cum. Don't stop."

With that, he puts a little more pressure on my clit and then starts pounding into me a little harder. His free hand grabs one of my tits, gripping me tight and pulling just enough to ride the line of pain and pleasure. With one hand on his shoulder and one gripping his thigh, I can't stop myself from digging my nails into him when my orgasm rushes through me. I feel his cock swell larger before he is cumming inside me.

He rolls to his back, taking me with him to lie on top of him. I kiss his chest while running my fingers over him.

"What is proper etiquette now?" I ask.

He smiles down at me. "Now you tell me I am the best you have ever had, and no man could ever compete with that. After that, you lie here while I run a bath for you to soak in. Then you let me rub your shoulders while I tell you that you are a fucking queen. Once all of that is done, you rest for a bit because I will be waking you up in a while for round two."

"Well, in that case, since you are the only man I have ever been with, I can confidently say that you are by far the best I have ever had."

James laughs.

"The rest of it sounds like a good plan. Scrub me, rub me, and tell me I'm pretty."

Chapter 17
James

"Jack, how is everything going up north? How are your classes going?"

"As good as they can be. I have one professor who I swear hates me. I have a solid 'B' in that class, and that's my lowest grade. It is what it is though, I suppose." Jack says.

"Well, keep your head up, Kiddo. I know you are doing your best, and I am proud of you."

"Thanks, Dad, how is everything going there?" Jack asks.

"Everything is going well. Betty has decided she will be retiring for good and she will be moving in with her oldest daughter next week. I am going to take over Lola duty for a bit until Reed finds a nanny."

"It's about time Betty retired! She's worked hard her whole life; I am sure Reed had Lola's energy on steroids when he was little. Where will she be living now? Still in town?" Jack asks.

I thumb through the papers on my kitchen counter. "No, but she is just moving a few hours north close to Jacksonville. Oh, and I convinced Reed to turn the garage over here into a gym since it will be a little harder to make it to the gym without having Betty around. I am looking through the blueprints now. I think you will be impressed if you ever make your way down here again to visit your feeble old man."

Jack scoffs. "Feeble my ass. Nice try with the guilt trip, Dad, but you would have to prove to be feeble to use that excuse. If my school load wasn't so heavy this semester, I would be down. But I am pretty swamped this semester and my next one. As soon as I can plan a visit, I will."

"I know, Kiddo. When you do come down, I have someone I want you to meet."

Jack laughs out, "Like a woman?"

I chuckle. "Yes, a woman."

"Sounds good, Dad. I am excited to hear about her. Unfortunately, I have to run. Tell me about her on our next call. I love you."

"I love you, too, Kid. Keep up the hard work and call me if you need anything," I say into the phone.

******

Walking into the main house, I am filled with sadness after packing Betty's bags into her daughter's minivan. I have worked for Reed for a few years now and Betty has been like a second mother to me. Especially when I was going crazy with Jack leaving for college. She became my sounding board when I wanted to drive up to South Carolina every other day to make sure my only child was okay and safe. Jack appreciates Betty being my voice of reason.

"My boys, I will spend every day I am gone worrying about you two. Reed, you are one of my own, pretty much, and I am so thankful for all you have taught me over the years- patience being the biggest thing," she says with a smile and a loving pat to Reed's cheek. "Jamesy my dear, I know you will keep this house running, but remember to take some time for you. Rely on your shell to keep you safe and warm," she says with a wink.

With a parting kiss to us, and then a five-minute, tear-filled goodbye with Lola, Betty leaves our home, and we all feel the immediate impact. When Gina left this house for the last time, no one was upset. Not one tear was shed by anyone. Betty leaving us though, feels like the heart of this home just stopped beating.

"How about you take tonight to go enjoy a night out. Go see a movie or something. I will stay home and take care of Lola. See you around noon tomorrow to meet with the contractors." Reed says with a pat to my shoulder.

"Sounds good. I will see you tomorrow. Need me to do anything before I go?" I ask.

"No, I think we all just need some downtime to work through Betty leaving. We will get on with our new normal tomorrow."

I nod my head. "Yeah, you are right. See you tomorrow." I grab my keys and head out to my car. Avery is supposed to be coming over in about four hours, but I will just head to her place. I don't want to be here right now. I need my shell, like Betty said.

******

Avery opens the door, dripping wet, with a small towel hanging loosely around her. "James? What's going on, are you ok?"

I step forward and wrap my arms around her. Pushing her into the house, I drop my head to her neck. "Betty just left, I need you."

She wraps her arms around my neck. "Honey, I am sorry."

"Just help distract me. Please?" I beg into her neck.

Avery jumps and wraps her legs around my waist. I feel the heat from her bare cunt against my shorts and I instantly get hard. My mouth finds hers, desperate for her lips. With one hand wrapped around her waist, I snake the other one up behind her neck, pulling her impossibly closer to me. I make my way to her bedroom and throw her onto the bed. With a bounce and a giggle, she gets up on her knees, crawling over to start undressing me. I grip the towel around her and yank it off.

"Damn, Dove, you are so fucking perfect," I growl.

Avery leans forward planting kisses all over me from my neck to my chest. I grip her hair, pulling her head up so I can kiss her plump lips.

Picking her up, I move us up her bed to the wrought iron headboard. "Put your hands here," I say, placing them on the lower bar. "And then," I say as I grab her feet and place them behind the highest bar and spread them as far as she can comfortably be, "keep these right here." I run my hands from her ankles down the back of her calves and then to her toned thighs before placing a hand on either side of her dripping wet pussy.

Avery stares at my hands with lust-drunk eyes as I begin massaging her mound in wide circles with my hands going in opposite directions.

Her head drops back. "James, more. Please. More."

I smile at her while I run one hand between her lips, pressing my thumb to her clit, teasing her with the rest of my knuckles. "I am getting there, Dove. Just getting you ready for me."

Her moans are the only response I get. Once I feel her body starting to get tense, I pull my hands away.

"James!" She yells, snapping her head to stare at me.

I lean forward and lick up her clit. "Yes, Dove?"

"If your plan is to tease me all night, I swear I will tie you to this bedframe and make you watch as I please myself. Hell, I will even leave you tied up the rest of the night so you can't do anything to please yourself."

I give her cunt another languid lick before swirling my tongue around her nub. "Patience, Dove." I move forward and lift her hips up long enough to place a pillow under them. "Do not let go of that headboard, do you hear me?"

She nods.

I grip her hips and slide into her tight, wet pussy. Her moans are fucking heavenly. The sight I have of me entering her is the hottest thing I have ever seen. The way she stretches around me is hypnotic. I look up to see her watching the view, too.

"Look at how fucking stunning your cunt is when it is wrapped around my cock, Dove. You were made for me. Only me." My thrusts into her are getting harder. "Can you feel how deep I am inside you?"

Avery nods frantically. "Yes, oh fuck yes. Harder James. Fuck me harder."

I do as she says, her perfect, bouncing tits are mesmerizing me. I smack her right tit before gripping it. "You want me to smack your pretty fucking tits again? I felt the way your pussy clenched around me just then." I smack her left tit this time.

"I'm going to cum, James. Do it again. Fuck! Do it again," she cries out.

I smack her right tit again and feel her pussy suck my cock in deeper as she cums. With two more thrusts, I spill myself into her as I have the strongest orgasm I have ever had. I help her lower her legs before wrapping myself around her.

"Do you want to watch a movie in here tonight?" she asks.

I kiss her shoulder. "Only if we can stay naked."

Avery rolls her head to face me. "You know Lucy is obsessed with you. Do you really want her to have access to your prized jewels there?"

I glance down. "Ok, we stay naked but under the sheets?"

Avery lets out a soft laugh, "You must be feeling invincible tonight. Suit yourself, or don't. Your balls, your call."

Once she has pulled up her movie of choice for the night, I pull her back into me and revel in the feel and smell of her.

******

The last few weeks have been a crazy mess of figuring out a new routine for all of us. The gym is nearly done. We have the room converted and most of our workout equipment is in. I held off on purchasing a few items when the owner of the gym I was attending had mentioned that he had plans to close in the near future. I suppose Betty wasn't the only one ready to move closer to her children.

Between Avery's other clients and Reed needing more help around the house with Lola, I have only been able to see Avery a handful of times; all brief and none of our normal overnights. Tonight will be our first night to have a night for just us in too long. I arrive at Peter's twenty minutes earlier than normal and am pleased to see that I am not the only one eager for tonight. Avery is already parked and standing outside of her Jeep.

She skips over to the golf cart. "What took you so damn long, old man?"

"Shut up and get your ass over here!" I growl at her.

She eagerly jumps in beside me and rests her hand on my leg. "Still on the hunt for a nanny? I may know a couple of girls looking for some full-time work. They are both working part-time jobs and needing a change."

"Really? Get me their contact information, and I will arrange an interview with Chris for them. While Lola is the apple of our eyes, I am ready to have a little free time to spend with you again. I have no turtle power without my shell these days," I joke as I squeeze her leg. "Oh, did you ever find that shirt that went missing the last time I was over there? Are you secretly holding it for ransom?"

"If I were going to hold any clothing for ransom, I would take that sweatshirt again. What use do I have for an old t-shirt? But no, I have not found it. My guess: aliens stole it. Maybe I have a poltergeist!"

"Of all the things for your poltergeist to steal: an old t-shirt? At least it has decent taste in clothing, I suppose," I joke as we pull up to the house

"So, what's on the agenda for tonight?" Avery asks when we walk inside.

"Did you want to check out the new gym? I know you like to work out but hate public gyms. You are welcome to squeeze in some time here on the nights you come over," I offer.

Avery's eyes light up. "Really? Let's go check it out. I would love to be able to get my workouts in with only one pervert staring at me compared to a roomful."

I glare at Avery. "Dove, do I need to start coming to the gym with you to make sure that no one is staring at my woman?"

"Sure, I suppose when you have a woman, that could be some new hobby you pick up," she jests.

"Run." I playfully glare at her. "You better run fast, Dove."

Avery lets out a giggle and then runs toward the door through my kitchen that leads to the garage-turned-gym. "You are too old to catch me, just give up now."

I lunge forward and grab her waist just as she reaches the door handle to the garage. Turning her to me, I whisper in her ear, "Never, Dove."

Her arms come up to wrap around my neck and I open the door to the gym. I back her in and when I feel like we are in a decent spot, I turn her around so she can take in the full view.

"We have a couple more things to get, but I think we did an okay job with the space. What do you think?" I ask.

"Looks better than my gym that I am paying an arm and a leg for! James, this looks amazing," she states as she takes it all in.

The wall-to-wall mirrors on the back wall, the treadmill, bike, vertical knee drop set up, plated weights, and kettle balls.

"We still have a few things that will be here next week that I got at a great price. But as for what is here, you are free to use anything you want."

Avery looks at me with hooded eyes. "Anything?"

I nod my head, "Yeah, anything."

She grabs my hand and leads me over to the vertical knee raise. Turning to face me, she leans up on her toes and kisses me softly. I grip her hips and pull her closer to me, growling into her kiss, but she pulls back from me. Never losing eye contact, she walks back against the machine, pulls her pants down and steps out of them.

"Fuck me then, James. I want to use you." She grips onto the handles and lifts her legs up, spreading them wide for me to settle in between them. I drop my pants without a second's hesitation and move forward to take my spot between her legs. Gripping her thighs, I slide my cock over her glistening cunt.

"Soaking wet for me already?"

"Don't make me regret my decision here, James. I can find another workout to reach my goal if you are too noisy," she says before nipping my lip.

I bite her lip back. "Oh, my little Dove, that's cute that you think I would let you out of this position you have put yourself into."

I thrust up into her, basking in the sight of her head rolling back and her moans slipping from her swollen and parted lips. With each thrust, I see her inching closer to her orgasm.

"Why so quiet now, my little Dove?" I ask mockingly.

"Shut up, James. Just. Fuck. Shut up and fuck me." Her lips crash against mine.

I pull my chest back from her and wrap her shirt collar around each of my fists. Without skipping a thrust, I rip her shirt down the middle.

With a gasp, she looks down. "Fucking hell, James, do that more often!"

I lock my eyes on hers, flatten my tongue, and slide from her hard nipple up her chest that is now covered in sweat, and up to her jaw. I can tell she likes it with the way her pussy is gripping my cock now.

"I am so close, James. So fucking close," she growls.

"You feel so damn good, Dove. So fucking good." I grip her thighs tighter as my thrusts start to become more erratic. Leaning my head against her collar, I bite down on the skin between her neck and shoulder.

Avery lets out a nonsensical string of words as her cunt clenches around me, making me cum instantly. As she lowers her legs, I kiss up and down her neck and face.

"So? Does the equipment live up to your standards?" I ask between kisses.

"Meh, makes a lot of noise," she says, smiling at me.

"Shut up, woman, and go pick our movie for the night," I say with a smack to her ass.

******

I am rubbing Avery's feet while she is sucked into the movie she picked tonight. "Oh, I forgot to mention, it looks like I will be having a work trip next month that I have to go on."

Avery looks at me. "North Dakota? Going to meet your little pinching vixen again so soon?"

I chuckle. "No, Illinois this time. Chicago, to be exact."

"Ohhhhh, the Windy City. When is that?"

"First weekend in June. We leave Friday and will be back Monday. Will you survive without me?"

"I don't know, that's an extremely long time. I could grow cobwebs, shrivel up, you never know," she jokes. "Oh, I won't be able to come over on one of our Sundays next month. I have a gala to attend."

"A gala?"

Avery nods her head. "Yeah."

"Do you need a date? I hear I look pretty decent in a tuxedo," I say playfully.

Avery glances at me nervously. "If I needed a date, I would definitely ask you to be mine. But, well, this is a work thing for me."

I rub my knuckle against her leg while I put together the questions I have. "So, you are going to this gala with a client of yours? On a date? In public?"

Avery shrugs. "Yes, with a client of mine. No, not a date. And yes, obviously in public. It is a gala to raise money for children with critical illnesses. Is this a problem?"

I tap my knuckle against her leg. "Correct me if I am wrong, but doesn't that break your fourth rule?"

Avery's eyes narrow in my direction. "Correct me if I am wrong, but I am pretty sure you bulldozed every rule I had, so I do not understand why me going to a children's fundraising event would not be acceptable."

I bite the inside of my lips to force myself to think before I answer her.

"And," she continues, "this is my job, James. My business that I began, so I believe that I can rearrange my rules as I see fit. Don't you? Especially since it is now April and you only paid me up through January. So, I suppose these days do not *belong* to you and are free for paying customers anyway."

I know better than to respond right now, but I ignore the logical part of my brain. "You can, and obviously the rules were never all that important anyway." This is when I realize I just fucked up.

Avery jumps to her feet, power walks over to the table by my front door and grabs her purse to leave.

"Where the hell are you going?" I ask, jumping up to stop her.

"Home."

"Get in here, Avery. Let's calm down and talk about this."

"Goodnight, James," she calls to me as she starts stomping down the walkway towards the tree line.

"Let me drive you to your Jeep at least," I say to her back.

Avery turns to me and throws a palm in the air. "I said goodnight, James."

I watch her turn around and begin walking away from me. I am mentally chastising myself for upsetting her as I run my hands through my hair. For making a big deal over a children's event. I am so stupid. I am just about to close the door when I hear Avery's scream. Her blood-curdling scream.

Chapter 18
Avery

"Who does he think he is? The absolute nerve! Arrogant son of a ... What the fuck?" I pause my spoken monologue to peer at whatever is standing in front of me in the shadows of the tree line. Squinting, I can see that it is long, whatever it is. Did I tempt fate about the alien thing because I am not down for probing.

Whatever the shadow is, it begins to move towards me with a deep growling sound. *Come on, brain, you have heard this sound, register it.* It only takes two more seconds of the sound and the thing moving nearly a foot closer, leaving barely ten feet between us for it to all register. That is a bellow. That is a bellow from an alligator. I let out a blood-curdling scream before my brain remembers that you need to stay calm in this situation. My scream was enough, though, to make the gator start moving and bellowing a little louder.

I turn and run as fast as I can towards James's house hoping his door is still unlocked. *Please don't let this be how I die.*

I am a couple of yards away when I see James looking around frantically. "Run! Run back into the house!" I yell at him.

He stops and looks at me.

"Jesus, James! For once, fucking listen to me! Runnnnn!"

He puts a pep in his step and runs back to his house. When I make it through the threshold, I slide as I turn to shut the door behind us as quickly as possible.

"What happened?" James asks as he runs his hands over my face and body. "You are as white as a ghost. What is it, Avery?"

Panting, I say, "An alligator. An alligator was chasing me."

James grabs his phone and hits a couple of buttons. "Hey boss, there is a gator in the yard by the trees. Don't let Lola come out here until we get animal control to come catch it. Sounds good, see you tomorrow." He grabs me and pulls me into his chest. "Are you okay?"

Still trying to catch my breath, I wrap my arms around him and nod against him.

"God, Dove, I was terrified when I heard you scream. I was so scared that something had happened to you, and I instantly hated myself for tonight. Please forgive me?" He begs against my cheek, trailing kisses between words. "I am such an asshole. You are right, I can't tell you how to run your business, and it was selfish of me to be upset over a children's gala. I am so sorry."

Even though I am shaken up by the alligator fiasco, his arms around me remind me why I was drawn to him from the first time I met him in the coffee shop. Though his mouth and mind run away from him at times, he feels like a safe place.

I cup his face. "Make it up to me, James."

And he does... many times that night. Soft and slow, hard and demanding, long and languid, deep and desperate.

******

I wake in the morning to hear James in the other room making breakfast. I stretch and slide into my favorite hoodie of his before making my way to the kitchen.

"Good morning, chef," I say as I stroll in.

"Just in time, sit down. I made some eggs, bacon and sliced up fruit. We are always rushing to get you home in the morning, so since we both have some time today, I wanted to cook for you," he says as he turns to face me.

I shake my head. "No need, I'm not hungry. You eat, though." Before the words fully leave my mouth, my stomach growls, betraying me.

James cocks his head to the side. "Did you just lie to me?"

I let out a loud sigh. "Look, I don't eat food that people make for me. It's not a discussion I want to have, alright?"

"Avery, this is a discussion we need to have. I need to understand."

I stand to head for the bedroom. "No, we absolutely do not need to have this discussion. I am going to get dressed and head back to my place. I am sure the gator has moved on by now."

"Avery."

That is all I hear before my panic attack takes over and everything goes black.

******

"One of these days I am going to be fooled into false security and it really will be the light at the end of the death tunnel," I say as I come to with a flashlight shining in my eyes.

"Avery, dear, we have to quit meeting under these circumstances," Peter starts, "you know the drill now. Any headaches? Vision issues?"

I shake my head. "No, I feel only slight embarrassment that you keep having to take care of me."

Peter swipes a hand through the air. "Nonsense, dear, it is rare that I get to put my house bag to use these days. You are keeping me on my old toes."

I sit up with a little help from Peter. "Well, at least you are staying on your toes."

Peter lets out a soft chuckle. "True. Gravity is not your friend, is it? You know the drill, dear. Twenty-four hours with no driving and you need to have someone with you."

I nod. "Yes sir. What do I owe you?"

Peter shakes his head. "Oh, nothing. You owe me nothing. Though I will never turn down an IOU just in case."

I smile at Peter and place my hand over his. "Well then, I have two IOUs with your name on them."

Peter clasps his other hand over mine. "I will save them for something good. You two have a good rest of your day. I will see myself back. Oh, and watch out, there is a gator on the loose. It's very vicious right now during mating season. He attacked my garden gnome this morning. Animal control should be by soon to try to take him to a home that is not mine."

James rushes over. "Avery, will you be alright while I run Peter home? It was in our yard last night; I don't want to risk you getting hurt now that I know it is still hanging around."

I nod my head and make a shooing motion. "Y'all go, I will be fine for a few minutes. I don't feel any concussion signs. Go on."

Peter walks over, grabs my hand and kisses my knuckles. "Get well soon, my dear, you know where I am if you need me."

"Thank you again, Peter. You are a doll."

When James walks back into his house fifteen minutes later, I am standing in front of the freezer and fridge, figuring out what I can make for myself. He doesn't say a word, just sits down with his breakfast and watches me while I pull out an orange and then reach into my purse to pull out an oatmeal packet I keep in there for emergencies such as this. Still, James doesn't push me on the subject again.

******

"We are twelve hours into the concussion hostage situation, what shall we do to occupy our time?" I ask.

James picks up his phone to check the time. "It's close to dinner time so why don't I cook something and we can put on a movie. How does that sound?"

I nervously rub my hands over my legs. "Or you can put a movie on and I will cook."

James wearily nods his head. "That works, but if we do this your way, I would like an explanation. We have been seeing each other for nearly a year now, Dove. I hope that I have earned your trust enough that you can talk to me about this."

I let out a huff and sit on the couch. "Okay. After dinner, I will tell you my story and you will tell me yours."

James throws out his hand. "Deal."

We make a quick trip over to my house to spend a little time with Lucy Fur for dinner and a movie.

******

After our dinner and a movie date, we drive back over to James's house for a sex-in-the-shower date. Once we are dried off and he has applied lotion to my entire body, we snuggle into his bed. I thought he had forgotten the deal we made, but I was wrong.

James lays his head on my stomach. "No more stalling, Dove."

I run a hand through his hair. "Okay. Give me a second to figure out where to start."

He wraps one of his arms over my thighs and the other one under them. "Take your time," he says before planting a kiss on my thigh.

I clear my throat and then bare my deepest and darkest secret to him. "I didn't want to move to Florida, but I was only thirteen when it happened, so my choice didn't exist. It didn't help that I was also the reason we were forced to move.

Colin was the hottest boy in our class. Jet black, messy hair, pale skin, amber eyes that nearly looked like honey, just walking around our middle school looking like a long-lost Cullen sibling. Somehow, the summer before eighth grade, I caught the attention of those amber eyes.

Our fathers worked for the same company. Colin's father was my father's boss, so we ended up at a lot of company parties together. It was at their cookout on the 4th of July where Colin made his first move on me. I was sitting on the wraparound porch of his house. I didn't want to be sitting further down in the yard where everyone else was; it was too crowded, too loud, and it hurt my ears. He came over and sat beside me, grabbed my hand, and we sat there watching the fireworks together. Of course, in my teenage mind, I was planning out our whole future-you know how teenagers are. Everything feels so significant at that age.

Over the rest of the summer, our parents would plan weekly outings for us all. Days out on the lake, baseball games, theme parks, horseback riding, anything you can think of. Every time he would become slightly more aggressive with his hidden displays of affection; pulling me in for a kiss that he didn't ask for, grabbing places he shouldn't. The first time he stuck his tongue in my mouth, I ran away and puked. My mom found me and thought it was just from the roller coasters.

When school started back up, we had a few classes together. I tried to sit across the room from him, but he would convince the teachers to move me to the desk right next to his. One day, I refused to sit by him and after class he yanked me out of my seat, pulled me into the bathroom, and screamed in my face. I vowed that I would never speak to him again and then I told my parents about what all had happened over the previous few months.

That night I heard my dad yelling at Colin's dad over the phone. The next day my dad was fired. Two days after that, my mother's access to the country club was revoked. Three days after that happened, my parents were called by the school nurse to pick me up early after I started vomiting and having convulsions. Obviously, my parents took me to the emergency department where they ran some blood work and found that I had ingested rat poison. I had eaten a cupcake that Colin had brought me that day. It had white buttercream frosting with pink sprinkles, sitting in a pink wrapper. I didn't think anything about it because he had brought some for everyone who usually sat at our table. The following week our house was packed, on the market, and we left Texas.

We tried to press charges, but since I ate the whole cupcake and had no proof that it was what poisoned me, nothing came of it. I am sure his dad's status in the community didn't help our side at all. But you know how it is in small towns: It's all about who you know and who you blow. That is how I ended up here."

James is staring at me in shock.

"So, that's my story. Now tell me yours," I say nonchalantly.

James squeezes his arms around my legs a little tighter. "Well, let's see: When I was eighteen, I was like any other young man and wanted to travel. The cheapest way to see the world was by joining the military. I went to tech school at Sheppard Air Force Base, where I had a drunken one-night stand that led to Jack. Jack's mom ended up choosing not to be involved in our lives shortly after Jack was born, and I never heard from or saw her again.

I didn't bother going through the courts or anything since I had no idea where she lived or even a phone number to reach her. We never dated. I went to all her doctor's appointments and paid for them. She would always call me from a payphone the night before an appointment to tell me when and where. I vowed to do right by that unborn child. I wanted to be a dad that any kid would be proud to have. Jack was about three months old when Vanessa knocked on my door, handed Jack to me, and left without a word.

We stayed at Sheppard for a few years, spent some time at Kirtland, a short stint at Lackland and then ended up here where I retired after my twenty years in the service. That is when I met my boss's dad. We were having my retirement party at this Italian restaurant on A1A and he and I ended up chatting and becoming friends. The week after my retirement, I was working for Mr. Ellingsworth, the senior, and when he passed a few months after, I stayed on to work for his son. Jack left to attend college in South Carolina a year and a half ago and I moved in here because it just made sense. So, I sold my big house, split the money between Jack and myself for our nest eggs, and here we are. Pretty boring."

I continue running my fingers through his hair. "I don't find that boring at all. Sheppard is right outside of my hometown. Maybe we met in the past and didn't even know it."

James nuzzles into my hand. "Please don't take this the wrong way, Dove, but I would have never given you a second glance if we had. I was a young adult; you were a child."

I let out a soft laugh and continue running my hand through his hair and down his face.

Our comfortable silence is broken by my phone ringing. "It's Sandy, I have to take this," I say as I stand and walk to James's living room.

"Hey, Peach," I say after answering.

"Oh my gosh, Aves! I am so glad you answered!" Sandy whisper yells.

"You are panting, are you okay?" I ask.

"Yes. No. I don't know. Physically, yes. I may end up on Snapped, but other than that, yeah, I am okay. No, no, I am not okay. I don't have to lie to you. I am not fucking okay."

I begin pacing the living room. "Alright, Peach, let's breathe in a big breath together and breathe out together."

"I can't, Avery. My heart hurts. My chest hurts. I can't believe I put up with that sorry asshole for so damned long! Why did you let me do this? You are supposed to be my friend in the scary movie who is like, 'Sandy, there is an alien on the back porch, so don't go out there or you will die.' But no! You sat by and allowed me to lose myself in his shit-ass orbit. If you weren't my only friend, I would knock you down to friend number two on my old Myspace."

I raise my pitch to feign shock, "Sandy Marie Sharie Nichole Bartholamew Brittany Darling, you go wash that mouth out with soap this instant!"

"Out of the five middle names you just used, none of them are actually mine. Spot three on my Myspace friends list," Sandy giggles out.

I smile even though she can't see me. "Ahhhhh, there she is. Welcome back from the edge of sanity, my friend. Now, tell me what happened in Tim's shit-ass orbit."

Sandy groans, "I just walked in on him with someone else."

I gasp. "No fucking way!"

Sandy sighs, "Yes fucking way. Is the offer still open for me to come your way? Make a new life as a Floridian? Get so tan I look like a leather bag sitting on the beach a decade from now?"

"Of course it is, Peach! I will prepare the office for your arrival. Lucy will be excited to officially meet her aunt."

Sandy lets out a soft chuckle. "Thank you for bringing me back to sanity. I will call you later to give you a time frame. I have a few things I need to wrap up here before I head that way. But will you keep this a secret for now?"

"Are you kidding me, you want me to keep a secret from Lucy Fur? You know she is the only one who could ever make it above you on my Myspace and I can't tell her about Tim proving to be a douche?"

"Okay, Lucy can know. But only her. I don't want to deal with people knowing what happened yet," Sandy laughs out. "I love you, Aves."

"I love you, too, Peach. Let me know when you know something."

I hang up and walk back into James's bedroom to find him in his sexy glasses, chest on display for my eyes to ravage, his night pants hanging low, and the book I brought over in his hands.

"Forget the other two girls I mentioned. I have your new nanny. Sandy is coming to stay with me. She's a perfect fit."

"We can chat more about that later. Let's do a story tonight, Dove," he says as he pats the bed beside him.

My smile takes over my whole face. "You are going to read Outlander to me tonight?"

"You and Betty both seem to like it, so it must be good," he says with a shrug.

I get into my cuddle position beside him, laying my head on his chest. "Well, the TV show gives you some great visuals, but the book is still the best."

James groans, "Oh yes, Betty told me all about Mr. Sam Heughan. Must be quite the looker to grab the attention of so many women."

I nod against his chest. "He sure is, but don't worry, you come in as a close second."

James pinches my ass and with a giggle, I cuddle in closer to him and listen as the voice that melts my heart reads to me about love, lust, and adventures.

Chapter 19
James

"Gwumpy! Awe you going to da zoo wiff ud today?" Lola asks as she skips through the kitchen.

"Sorry, Princess Unfortunately, I have responsibilities that I need to handle today. Can I make it up to you another day?" I ask sincerely.

Lola takes a second to think it over. "I duppode you can wiff ice cweam watew."

"I bet I can handle that," I say to her as I lead her to the table with her yogurt and fruit for breakfast. I hear the back door open and turn to see Christine walking in. "Chris, just the woman I want to see!"

Chris sets her stuff down on the counter. "Good morning. Is this a conversation I will be happy to have before coffee, or should we put a pin in it for about fifteen minutes?"

I grab a couple of coffee mugs from the cabinet. "I may have found our nanny. She comes highly recommended from a friend I trust. She is moving in from out of town, so I don't know the exact date as of yet, but it will be soon."

Chris drops to her knees in a mock bow. "James, I am not worthy of your gifts to me." She stands and straightens her slacks. "But for real, you just saved me the biggest headache of interviewing a ton of people. I will just interview the highest qualified I have on my list for now, in case your person doesn't want the job."

I nod to Chris. "Sounds like a plan, but I don't think she will turn us down. I take it you are the zoo chaperone today?"

Chris waves her hand over her ensemble of black slacks, a white cotton tank, and white tennis shoes. "I am in my casual clothes, James, where did you think I was going?"

I cough out a laugh. "You and I have very different definitions of casual." I look down to emphasize my jeans and old t-shirt.

Chris throws her thick red hair over her shoulder. "Unlike you and Reed, I haven't given up on finding a soulmate. Therefore, I have to always look presentable. Never know when *the one* will find me and all that jazz."

I pass Chris her coffee. "You would look beautiful in a potato sack."

Chris laughs. "Don't go all dad on me, James, you know it makes me weepy. Come on, Princess, let's go see how big the gorilla's belly is now."

I kiss both girls on the head before shooting a text off to Reed to let him know I will be running errands today and that I am taking the truck, so he is stuck with my car for the day. I have to go buy a bed and a few other things to get Avery's house ready for Sandy. I wasn't going to pass up getting to spend more time with her- especially since our time will be more limited now that I can't just show up at her house when I want to.

***

Tonight is my last selfish night with Avery for a while. Sandy arrives tomorrow and we know that the next few weeks will be hit or miss on when we will get to see each other. I spent the last week and a half waiting to surprise her with what I have planned for us tonight. Is it a little manipulative of me? Probably. But I knew that I had to be smart with my timing for this.

After a quick glance around the house, I run out to jump on the golf cart. I still haven't found the hole in the fence line, but I haven't looked too closely either. If Sandy decides to take the nanny job, I will crack down on the fence once some of my time is freed up from her being here with Lola. My daily honey-do list is longer than a Walgreens receipt and only gets longer with each passing day.

Pulling up to Peter's driveway and seeing Avery leaning against her Jeep takes all the stress and overthinking away. She skips over to the golf cart and slides into her spot next to me.

She kisses my cheek. "Mmmmm, looking like a hunk today."

"Not too shabby yourself," I say while slipping my hand between her thighs.

"What's on the agenda tonight?" she asks.

I squeeze her thigh. "Well, I figured a movie, an orgasm or five to hold us over, and a small surprise that I planned for us."

"You know I don't love surprises," she laughs out.

I park the golf cart. "I know. Get your ass in the house." I really hope this doesn't backfire on me because I need this to work.

When we walk in, I tense up and wait for her reaction. When she spots what is out on the counter in my kitchen, she turns to me with a glare.

"If you wanted Peter to hang out tonight, you could have just called him. This seems like a really extreme way to get him to come over," Avery says as she crosses her arms over her chest.

I point to the ingredients out on the counter. "I don't want to see Peter. I want you to take back your power while simultaneously handing a little of your trust over to me, Dove. Tonight, we are baking cupcakes…together."

Avery nervously shakes her head. "I don't think I want to do this."

Now for the part that I knew would come and could blow up in my face. "Okay, well, I will be baking them then. You can stay and eat one, or you can go. I won't force you to stay."

Avery's mouth drops open. "What? It is our last night together for a bit, and you are fine with me leaving over cupcakes?"

I shake my head. "Nope, I am not fine with it. But I don't control you, and I have to bake these for Lola tonight. She needs them for a tea party she was invited to tomorrow."

"Then I don't need to eat one. Bake away."

I shake my head again. "I do need you to eat one, though. I had a dentist appointment today and I have to lay off the sugars until I go back."

"Cavity?" she asks.

I shrug.

Avery looks around nervously. "James, the pink sprinkles, the pink wrappers. You know. I told you."

"I know, Dove, and I am sorry. I was told what to get and didn't have a say in the colors. You can do this. We can do this. It will make one little four-year-old girl the happiest girl in the world."

Avery rolls her eyes. "I never knew that you would throw out some low blows like that. Using a child to get your way. Fine. Let's do this."

We spend the next hour in the kitchen baking, frosting, decorating, and dancing. One of Avery's stipulations for baking this was that we had to listen to pop songs of the early 2000s. She said it reminded her of when she and Sandy would bake with Sandy's dad. The way Avery talks about Sandy's dad, you would think it was her own father rather than her best friend's father.

By the time the cupcakes are done, Avery is so relaxed from her dancing and storytelling that she does not even hesitate to grab a cupcake, remove the pink wrapper and take a bite. That is, until she sees me staring with a shit-eating grin on my face.

Avery looks down at the cupcake in her hand and then up to me, tears in her eyes. "I just took a bite of this. James, I just took a bite of this cupcake without even thinking."

I move from my spot leaning against the counter and walk to stand in front of Avery. Wiping away her tears, I smile at her. "You just took a bite of a cupcake with white buttercream frosting, pink sprinkles, and a pink wrapper around it that someone else also made."

Avery looks up at me with tears still in her eyes and whispers, "I love you."

I grab either side of her neck. "I love you, my little Dove."

I lean down for a soft kiss, but Avery has a different plan in mind. Latching her arms around my neck, she jumps up to wrap her legs around my hips. I grab her ass when she does. Turning, I set her on the clear counter. Her legs tighten around me, and her arms pull my head closer to hers.

"Show me how much you love me, James," Avery pants out.

I pull her down from my counter and turn her around so her back is against my chest. Slowly, I lift her short dress up over her head to find her braless and in a flimsy thong. I run my hands over her ass, her back, and around to cup her tits before moving one hand down to tease her thong-covered pussy.

"Spread your legs," I growl into her ear before trailing kisses and bites down her neck and shoulder.

Without hesitation, she obeys. Looping my finger around the small triangle of fabric over her mound, I pull it to the side with one hand while releasing my cock with my other hand. I push lightly on Avery's back to force her to lean over the counter as I loop my arm around her left knee and lift it, grabbing the countertop to keep her leg in the air.

Avery reaches down, grabbing my cock before aligning me with her dripping cunt and sinking back onto my throbbing dick. "Oh my, yes. I need you. I need you so bad."

I pick up my thrusting. "Be a good girl and rub your clit for me."

Avery glances at me over her shoulder before reaching between her legs and doing as I told her. With a moan, she drops her head to the counter. I can tell she is getting close by the way her muscles in her back are starting to tighten. I put a little more crouch in my stance so I can hit her G-spot.

"Fucking A, yes. Mmmmmm right there, don't stop. Please, don't stop," Avery pants.

Her moan when she cums nearly does me in, but before I can finish, she lowers her leg and turns to face me. Pushing me back against the island, she grabs the icing and drops to her knees in front of me. Looking up and into my eyes, she sticks her hands in the remaining icing and spoons out some before trailing it along the head of my dick.

"Little Dove, are you still hungry?"

She seductively sucks one of her fingers into her mouth and then, with a pop, pulls it out. "I want more dessert."

I wrap her hair around my hand so I can enjoy the view she is about to give me. Her eyes never leave mine as she takes as much of me into her mouth as she can. I drop my other hand to her throat. She reaches up to grab my balls, and within seconds, I feel my orgasm rushing through me. Feeling her swallow my cum down with my hand resting on her throat is one of the sexiest feelings I have ever felt.

I help her stand and get myself situated back in my pants before grabbing her dress and sliding it over her head. While she is getting her dress situated, I come behind her to kiss her shoulders and neck again.

"I really do love you, Little Dove."

Avery hums and leans back into me. "I really do love you, too, Honey."

"So, are you willing to be my girlfriend yet?" I ask.

Avery turns to look me in the eyes and cups my cheek. "I love you. I am only intimate with you. But I don't know that I am ready to put a label on this."

I drop my eyes to the ground and nod out of habit.

Avery stoops low so I am forced to see her eyes again. "It is not because I don't want to be with you, James." She begins to stand to her full height again and I keep my eyes on hers. "It is that I have commitments that I have already made and it would be unfair to you for me to be in someone else's bed, even if it is strictly platonic. I already act as a girlfriend would with you and I am in no way available for anything from anybody else. But I just need more time before we label this."

Though I don't like her answer, I understand to an extent. "You could just quit. I can support us while you find something else you would like to do."

Avery leans in and gives me a deep kiss.

"Unfair woman, using your mouth to distract me," I growl out before biting her bottom lip.

She smiles softly. "I think we have had a lot of big things happen tonight and should leave making big decisions for a different night. I want to get my shelling on with a musical."

"Go get the movie loaded, I'll tidy up in here and then meet you in there in a minute."

******

Last night was spent cuddling with a movie and Avery falling asleep on the couch. When I moved her to my room, she did her typical starfish and took up most of the bed, so I got my normal sliver of a spot. While I am excited to have more room on the bed, I am not looking forward to not having her with me.

I am pulled from my inner thoughts when my phone rings. I set my teacup down. "Excuse me, Princess, I must take this."

Lola waves her hand over the table. "You awe excwuded Gwumpy."

I stand up from her kiddie table and step a few feet away before answering Avery's call.

"Hello, Dove, miss me already?"

Avery's laugh warms me. "Of course I miss you already. But that is not the reason for my call. Did you happen to get a time from your lady friend about when I need to have Sandy at the coffee shop tomorrow? I forgot to ask you before I left."

"Yeah, she said she can meet you at our coffee shop at ten."

"Sounds like a plan. Thank you again for setting this all up. What are you up to right now?" Avery asks.

"Oh, not a lot. You know, the usual. I am at a tea party with the Princess."

Avery scoffs. "There was no tea party invite, was there?"

I scoff back. "Excuse me? Are you calling me a liar? Lola was invited to a tea party today. I know because I was the one who invited her. Now, if you don't mind, Miss Judgeypants, I have a princess awaiting my return."

Avery lets out a heavenly sounding laugh. "I love you."

A smile takes over my face. "I love you too, Dove. Call me when you get a chance."

I hang up and head back to my seat.

"Please forgive me for my absence, Princess. It was my Queen," I say to Lola.

"Fogwiven, it id a dame youw queen couwdnt join ud," she says seriously.

I nod. "Shame, indeed. Cheers."

We tap our teacups before digging into our cupcakes.

Chapter 20
Avery

I am shaking my ass in the kitchen with Celine going through my little portable speaker. I am lucky that I woke up with a minimal hangover after last night's rum and purge session with Sandy. I bet my body just metabolized the alcohol quickly because I had so much adrenaline pumping through my body after hearing what Tim did. I would love to force-feed that boy a knuckle sandwich or two after what he did to my best friend.

When Sandy joins me in the kitchen for some Celine sing-alongs, my mood jumps from normal-meh to excited. I didn't realize how much I missed her after being away from each other for so long. I feel that between her and James, my life is pretty whole now. I am still not ready to tell anyone about James or about how we met, though. Bartending has been a good cover for my job and I want to keep it that way. It is more than just my feelings to consider with that choice.

After our kitchen concert and breakfast, we break apart to get ready for the day. I throw on a bikini with a pair of shorts and a tank top before heading back to the living room to wait for Sandy. I check my work emails and find one from Cal.

Avery,

While I was out and about, I picked up a dress for you for the gala. I went with a lavender color, so base your shoes and makeup off of that. I will show it to you when I see you next. I am thinking of a grey suit for myself with a tie that matches your dress. Can't wait to see you.

Cal

Ughhhhhhh, I am beginning to regret agreeing to going to the gala. I would rather spend that night with James, but I have already committed to this. When Sandy walks in, I make a twirling motion with my hand. I am so happy to see my best friend looking confident with her signature, big smile. "Alright, Peach, get your cute little ass in the Jeep. Let's blow this popsicle stand and start the new and improved version of your life."

******

While Sandy is in her interview, I use this time to give James a quick call.

"My little Dove, miss me already?"

I laugh out, "Yes. I realized that I didn't wake up to a smart ass remark or an orgasm, so I figured I would call you to get at least one of them out of the way for the day."

"So, you want to have phone sex to get your morning orgasm? I am in the middle of the grocery store at the moment, but I could kill a couple birds with one stone if I talk loudly enough. The women trailing me in here would probably appreciate it," James laughs out.

"You dirty old man. I was actually calling for the smart-ass remark. Once Sandy is done with Chris, we are heading to the beach. I don't think you want me all hot and bothered around a bunch of half-dressed men," I joke.

"Hmm, sounds like I need to change my plans for the day and carve out some time to stuff your mouth so you don't make empty threats like that again," he states.

"Morning quota filled. Thanks, Honey. Gotta go. Love you," I rush out before hanging up on him.

Sandy is still in the coffee shop, so I should email Cal back while I am just sitting here.

Cal,

Sounds lovely. I can't wait to see what you picked out. I could have found a dress myself, but I appreciate your initiative. I have quite a selection of shoes that could work with a lavender dress. I will bring them over on my next night with you so we can go through them together to check our heights with them on. You know how snap-happy photographers get at galas. See you in a few days.

Avery

I see Sandy and Chris walking towards the door, so I flip through my many playlists to find my "Girls of Summer" playlist. I am going to make sure this girls' day starts off right for us.

"So? Did you wow her?" I ask when Sandy sits down in the passenger seat.

Sandy gives me a solemn look.

"What? No way! I know there is no way that you were not offered this job!" I screech out.

Sandy's solemn look slowly changes, and a shit-eating grin takes over her face. "I start tomorrow."

I fist bump the air and start screaming, "Woooo hoooo! I knew you would get it!"

Sandy looks around and notices that people are watching us now. "Avery, shhhhh."

I wave her off. "You shhhh. Let's go get celebratory shots. You have four blocks to change into your bathing suit."

"Here in the Jeep?" Sandy squeaks out.

"Yes, here in the Jeep. The back windows are tinted, slide back there."

******

Once our umbrella and towels are set in place for our beach day, I convince Sandy to promenade around the beach with me. In my mind, we are Elizabeth Bennet and Caroline Bingley, but instead of walking around a small room, we have the sun and sand enveloping us. A few minutes in, I notice a blond beach boy and his dark-haired, brooding, Mr. Darcy friend watching us.

"Sandy, he keeps glancing over here! Push your chesticles up, Peach. And fix that frown. Gosh, your lips and nips are pointing the same direction right now. Down.

We can't have that. Come here." I say as I reach into Sandy's bikini to make her boobs look happier.

"Aves, let's go grab a cocktail from the pier. I don't think I am ready to go hit on guys yet, and I won't be ready to do that without a little liquid courage. Just no rum. Probably no tequila either."

We start heading towards the pier. "Ok, Sandy, today you are not Sandy. You need to build your confidence back up. I need my best friend back, not just this shell of her. Is she still in there?"

"Ok then, Aves, who am I today? A secret agent on a special mission? Looking for James Bond only to find Austin Powers with my luck?"

I can't help but laugh. "No, Peach, today you are Dolly. You are my busty, southern blonde. You have not a care in the world. You do not care what anyone else thinks about you because you are beautiful as you are. Drag queens want to be you, and women want your nonexistent man. As long as you don't run into Jolene today, you are safe. So, let's grab our drink, Dolly. This is our day, and we are going to carpe the fuck out of this diem."

"If I am Dolly, then who are you?" she asks me.

"Oh, honey, today I am Cher circa 1973. I can't let you be the only one admired by our Queens."

******

Back at our beach spot, cocktails in hand, I glance around to see that blond beach boy is still staring our way. I am so lost in thought staring at him that I didn't immediately notice the guy who fell on Sandy. I jump up to get him off of her, but the dude used half a vat of tanning oil and I can't get a decent grip on him. *Did this guy use tanning oil or straight lard?* Suddenly, our brooding beach Darcy swoops in like a white knight and knocks the oiled-up loser off of Sandy.

"I thought my boobs were going to crack my rib cage," Sandy says.

247

"Dolly… Dolly, can you hear me?" I ask her.

"If I could turn back time…" is all she responds with.

I can't stop the laugh that escapes me as I lean in to pry her eyelid open and help her sit up.

"Sorry, fella, I'm not ready to go today," she says to Beach Darcy.

I am starting to get a little concerned. Did that guy land on her head? Beach Darcy is running his hands over her head and neck while asking her questions that she is not answering. I can feel my anxiety creeping up and then the blond beach boy puts a calming hand on my shoulder. I look back at him to see him giving me an "it will all be okay" kind of look. I am lost in his look until I hear Sandy's voice again.

"I'm ok, I think. What the hell happened? I was reading and then, oh shoot! My book. Where is my book?"

I point out to the water where her book is floating further into the ocean.

"Well, if no one has an answer, I am going to go grab a drink. I think I deserve one after whatever that was," she says as she stands.

Beach Darcy stands up. "I'll walk with you to make sure you are okay. I will tell you what we saw along the way. Sound like a plan?"

Sandy looks at me and I make a shooing motion for her to go. I need a moment to nip this anxiety attack that is building. I turn to cover my face but notice that the blond is still kneeling next to my towel and staring at me intently.

"You are more than welcome to go with them. I will be fine here on my own," I state.

Blondie nods. "I could, but I saw something that caught my eye and now I just can't draw myself away from it."

I snort. "Wow, does that pick-up line ever work for you?"

Blondie cocks his head to the side. "Pick up line? Oh, my vain, little beauty, I was talking about that necklace."

I grab my necklace protectively. "It is lovely, isn't it?" I ask wearily.

Blondie nods. "It is. It is still as lovely as the day I went with my new friend to pick it up." Blondie cocks an eyebrow up and lowers his glasses. "He did tell me it was for a gorgeous woman, but he never mentioned that you were a young and gorgeous woman."

I grip my necklace a little tighter. "And what exactly did he tell you?"

Blondie pushes his glasses back up and looks out to the water. "Not much, just that he had been seeing this total babe and needed to know who I would recommend to find such a stunning piece of jewelry. Had he wanted simple diamonds, that would have been a breeze. Finding a jeweler to make the turtle with that ruby actually made me use some brain power. It looks stunning on you."

I look down at the turtle in my hand and blush. "I agree. Thank you for helping him find the perfect gift for me."

"No, thank you. I went from being annoying to useful to him. So where is my friend at? Why is he not here protecting his woman from the starving eyes of all the men on this beach?" Blondie asks with his arms out to emphasize how many people are at the beach today.

"Last I heard, he was being followed by a gaggle of geriatric women at the grocery store," I say with a shrug.

Blondie nods his head. "Hmmmm. Well, I will have to let him know what a dumb idea it was to allow such a beauty to be out without her beast to ward off these villagers."

I chuckle out, "You do that, bud. He will probably laugh at the thought of me being some meek woman who needs his protection."

I glance over to see Sandy and Beach Darcy standing at the foot of our towels, drinks extended to me and blondie.

I take and raise my cup. "Well, I say this calls for a toast. Thank you, gentlemen, for saving my Dolly here and thank you for the booze. Tonight, we're going down in flames. Just like Jesse James."

******

Sonny and Carl, aka Blondie and Beach Darcy were a fun distraction for a bit, but I was excited when Sandy was ready to go home. While she was in the shower, I gave James a quick call.

"Two phone calls in one day? You must really be missing me," he coos through the line.

"I met a friend of yours today," I state.

"Oh yeah? Who might that be?" James asks.

"Sonny."

"Sorry, Dove, I don't know a Sonny," he says.

"Hmmm, young thirties, blond, hits the gym and the beach a lot judging by his tanned muscles. He mentioned helping you pick out my necklace."

James sighs. "Oh, you met Brad. Why would he say his name was Sonny?"

I let out a soft chuckle. "Probably because I said my name was Cher."

"Yeah, that would do it," James laughs out. "Was he a gentleman at least?"

"Yeah, him and some guy that I am guessing is not named Carl were polite. Not Carl saved Sandy when some greased up goon fell on her," I say while twirling the string of my bikini top.

"Was this 'not Carl' a brunette guy with green eyes?" James asks.

"Winner, winner chicken dinner," I say.

James chuckles. "Well, sounds like you met my boss, Reed."

I sit up straight. "No shit. Oh, I can't tell Sandy or she won't show up to work tomorrow. She would die of embarrassment. We never had this conversation."

"Whatever you say, Ring Mistress. I miss you."

I sigh. "I miss you, too. Sandy just shut off the water. Gotta go. I love you."

Chapter 21
James

"I love you, too, Little Dove," I get out before ending the call.

I make a mental note to corner Brad and find out exactly what he said to Avery today. With Lola being at her mom's and Reed being out of the house, I have taken this free time to get some of my list dwindled down so that I can fit in some Avery time this week. I figured while Sandy is here at the house, I can sneak away to at least kiss Avery. I am missing her way more than I should.

When I see Brad's truck coming up the driveway on the monitors, I jog to the golf cart and head up to the main house.

Brad waves at me as I pull up closer. "Hey, old man, fancy seeing you here."

Reed shakes his head. "I'm going to go shower. Beers and pizza tonight?"

"Yeah," I say.

"Sounds perfect," Brad says.

Once Reed is in the house, I turn to Brad. "So, Carl, how was your day at the beach?"

Brad crosses his arms across his chest. "Full of beautiful sights to see. Especially this one total hottie," Brad snaps his fingers. "Cher was her name, I think."

I lick my lip and nod. "Ahhhh, Cher, she is quite a sight. If you want to keep yours, I'd suggest keeping your sights off her."

Brad throws his hands in the air. "No need for empty threats. I saw the turtle on the chain around her neck before I did or said anything stupid. Your girl is safe. I will only look at her as a sibling from here on out, Pops."

I can't help but laugh. "Oh God, please never call me 'Pops' again."

"What? Any man of your age would love to have me as a son or son-in-law," Brad says, puffing out his chest.

I shake my head. "I'd rather take a bullet than have to put up with you as either."

Brad throws a hand over my mouth. "Don't speak that kind of negativity into the universe, man!"

I remove his hand. "Go get ready for dinner. I will call in the pizzas. Oh, and Brad, what did you think of the new nanny?"

Brad looks at me quizzically. "Dolly? No fucking way!" Brad throws his hands up in the air. "Shit's about to get soooo good." Brad jumps forward and kisses my cheek. "Thank you for the early birthday gift, old man! Oh, he has no idea, does he?"

I wipe my cheek. "No, none at all."

******

By Monday, I am going through Avery withdrawals. After I made breakfast for everyone, I hauled ass out of the house to make it to the coffee shop for our date. I would much rather be at her house or mine so I can do everything I want to do to her, but I will take what I can get at the moment.

I walk in the door and see her sitting at our normal table. My heart beats harder as I walk over to her.

"Is this seat taken?" I ask her.

Avery coyly tucks her hair behind her ears. "Well, I was waiting on someone, but you are way more handsome than he is, so please do sit down."

I lean over the table and give her a hard and demanding kiss. "Good answer. How is your morning going?"

"Well, considering I woke up to Brad stinking up my house from his disgusting boy farts, it is going rotten. Well, that was until you walked in."

"And why was Brad at your house this morning early enough to wake you up?" I ask.

Avery giggles. "We took Sandy out dancing last night to celebrate her first day on the job. Apparently, Reed kissed her so good that she lost a little bit of her sanity. Anyway, she was dancing with this guy who I can't say for sure drugged my friend's cousin, but was definitely at the bar the same night it happened and she danced with him that night. Regardless, Sandy was looking cozy with him and it stirred up some emotion in me that I didn't like. Maybe a sixth sense or something, I don't know. Brad and I grabbed a bunch of shot glasses from other tables and pretended to be hammered by the time she came back from the dance floor. To hold up appearances, he crashed on my couch."

"That's a lot to take in."

Avery sips her coffee. "I know, right? How is your morning?"

I wrap my hands around the coffee she had sitting at the table for me. "I woke up thinking about this sexy-as-hell woman, rubbed one out, made some pancakes, watched our nanny get doused in coffee, and then walk around in my boss's shirt. I am pretty sure he has the hots for the new nanny. Now I have the pleasure of sitting in front of my masturbation muse." I shrug feigning nonchalance. "So, it has been a good morning, I suppose."

Avery stands and grabs my hand. "Let's run to my house and make it a little better."

******

Walking through the front door, I was hoping to sneak into a bathroom to clean up a little, but I am startled by a little dark-haired girl holding a Post-it in one hand and a pen in the other.

"Gwumpy, can I take youw owdah?" Lola asks, already scribbling on her Post-it.

"We are about to make some sandwiches for lunch, what kind would you like?" Sandy asks me.

I glance between Lola and Sandy while I pretend to think about what I want. "Hmmmm, I think a turkey with all the fixings sounds like a good choice. What do you think, ma'am?"

"I dink it id a good pick, Gwumpy, good pick indweed," Lola says, continuing her scribbles.

"Perfect, I am just going to freshen up and I will be right there," I tell the girls before sauntering down the hall and past the kitchen to the guest bathroom.

When I walk into the kitchen a few minutes later, I see Lola sitting at the table, Sandy at the counter making a sandwich, and Reed staring at the ceiling. I can see that things have not simmered down since this morning. The frustration on Reed's face hides nothing and I can't stop myself from smirking at him.

"Ms. Sandy, here are your clothes. They just finished, so I grabbed them on my way through the laundry room," I say, setting her clothes on the counter and then turning to the fridge for a drink.

"James, you are the best. I am almost done with your sandwich, just have to add the lettuce. Go take a seat, and I'll bring it over in a second," Sandy says, and I do as I am told.

******

I'm heading back over to my place after lunch when my phone starts ringing.

"Miss me already, Dove?"

Avery laughs out, "I do, actually. Also, my night just opened up; my client cancelled. Want to pick me up at our meeting spot? Same time as usual?"

I shake my head, even though she can't see me. "I wish I could, Dove, but tonight is a no-go for me. I have a video chat with Jack tonight and then some work I have to get prepped that Reed needs for a meeting he has tomorrow. His new nanny has him all sorts of distracted, you know, so I have to pick up the slack," I chuckle out.

"Bummer about the boss, but I hear the new nanny is a total hottie with a body so I can't blame him. Cool with you if I hit a bonfire with our new mutual friend?" Avery asks.

"You mean your idiotic neighbor? Not the cool old guy with the dog, I mean the one on the other side of him. The blond bimbo?" I ask jokingly.

"Yeah, that one. Apparently, one of his school friends is throwing a spring break bonfire. If it is weird for you, I will stay home. I know that he is the only one who knows about us- well, besides Betty, since you need multiple people to help you pick out gifts and whatnot...."

"Are your gifts to your satisfaction?" I ask.

"Yes, you know they are James," she whispers.

"Then they did their jobs well. It is called delegating, Dove," I joke. "But go, have fun. It won't be weird for me. I can sleep easier knowing that you are with someone I know and can find if anything happens to you."

Avery snorts. "Oh, I love when you go all macho protective and shit. It's hot. We should role-play that next time I see you."

I smile. "Anything you want, Dove. I have to run. I love you."

"Love you too, Honey!"

Chapter 22
Avery

Sitting around the beach bonfire, my rum in hand, I am wishing I was at home and in his arms. Brad is good, fun company per usual, but one guy at the bonfire has decided I am his intended target for the night and I am already over it. I have politely declined his offer to go for a walk, to dance under the stars, go for a quick dip in the ocean, and now the tool has decided to take up residence on the blanket next to me. He is giving me Colin vibes with his 'can't-take-no-for-an-answer' attitude. Brad is escorting one of his female coworkers to the bathroom up by the parking lot, so I am trying to just ignore Colin 2.0 as best I can.

"So, how about you give me your number and I can set up a date for us this weekend? I know the owners of a place on the mainland that is great. The food is amazing," Colin 2.0 says to me.

I turn my head in the opposite direction and can't hide my smile when I see a familiar face sauntering up to me.

"Sorry, Josh, she already has plans this weekend. She is my date for the gala," Cal says as he sits down beside me and kisses my cheek.

Colin 2.0, or Josh, I suppose, puffs out his chest. "Cal, good to see you, but I think it should be her decision. A boring gala or a dinner at a classy restaurant with a three-month wait to get in where I can pull some strings to get us in this weekend. Gorgeous?" Josh asks as he reaches out to rub a finger down my face.

Cal grips Josh's hand before it touches me. "Sorry, old sport, I am afraid she already made the commitment." Cal drops Josh's hand and looks at me. "Unless you truly don't want to go, then you are free to do as you please."

I wrap my hands around Cal's biceps and turn to face Josh. "Yeah, sorry, old sport. I plan to keep the date I already have. I am sure you can find someone here who would love to join you, though."

Josh stands with a grumble and walks away from us.

I sigh. "Oh, thank you! He has been annoying me all night," I whisper to Cal. "Wait, what are you doing here? I thought you had to work tonight."

Cal shakes his head. "No, all I said in my email was that I had to cancel." Cal points to Brad's coworker who is throwing this shindig. "That's Callie, my twin sister. I was not about to let her come out here without me knowing that creepy Josh was coming. That is why my email was so last-minute. She just told me today about Josh catching her at the store and inviting himself when she told him she was throwing a beach party. He was our neighbor growing up and he always gave me the creeps. I have never liked the way he looks at Callie. He uses the "I'm a bartender" excuse to invite himself to parties all of the time; not that he ever mixes any drinks while he is at them."

I raise an eyebrow. "Cal and Callie?"

Cal huffs out a laugh. "Yeah. Calvin and Calliope. Her name means beautiful voice; my name means bald. Can you tell Mom was more excited about having a girl?"

"How did I not know that you were a twin?" I ask him.

Cal shrugs. "You never seem to want to share or know intimate details. I am surprised you don't get annoyed with me talking about work so much, but that's the only thing I have to talk about besides my family."

I lay a hand on Cal's arm again. "Cal, I am your friend. Of course I want to know about your family, too. I am sorry that I never showed that. I promise to be a better friend immediately. What can I do to prove it to you?"

Cal leans over and kisses my forehead. "Just keep being you, Gorgeous."

"And who might this be?"

I look up to see Brad standing over us with his arms crossed over his chest.

"Brad, this is my friend Cal. Cal, this is Brad," I say, waving my hand respectively between them.

Cal extends a hand to Brad. "Nice to meet you, Brad, I am Callie's brother. I have heard many great things about you from my sister."

Brad grips Cal's hand. "It is nice to meet you, too. She is a pretty spectacular nurse. She really connects with all her students and takes great care of them. So, how do you two know each other?"

I put my hands on Cal's shoulders. "Work," I say simply. I have made it very clear to Brad that I won't talk about my work with him. He knows it isn't bartending like I try to sell, but he doesn't know anything more than that.

Brad nods his head. "Well, that is nice, Avey Davey. You about ready to head out? It's getting late, and I don't want us waking up Sandy when we get home."

I smirk at Brad's implication that we are going to the same house. "Sure." I turn to Cal and lean in to give him a hug. "See you Sunday," I whisper in his ear.

Cal smiles at me. "Yeah, see you around. It was nice to meet you, Brad."

Brad loops his arm in mine and begins leading me to his truck. "Do I need to be worried about my friend's heart over that guy?"

I laugh out, "You are a few months too late on that one. What is it with you guys and Cal? Are his looks really that threatening?"

Brad whips his head to me. "Threatening? No. I won't deny that I never plan to stand next to him, though. On my own, I would say I am a solid 9 in the looks department, but next to him, I would be a 2. Who are his parents? George Clooney and Cindy Crawford? It makes sense, though; Callie is probably the most gorgeous woman I have ever laid eyes on, but I have a strict 'don't stick your pen in company ink' rule, so she is pretty much a man in my eyes now."

I shake my head. "You are something else, my friend."

******

"No wonder Avery calls you Peach."

"Avery, shut off your alarm clock. He is annoying."

I roll out of bed and waddle into the living room. "Brad, quit staring at her cute little ass. I might get jealous or something."

I didn't get home from Theo's until nearly four this morning. He was having a really bad night, and it took a while for Beth and me to get him calmed down.

"What is going on that you decided to grace us before seven in the morning on a Sunday?" Sandy asks.

"Throw some pants on. No need to get dressed up on my account, but make it quick. I have a surprise for the two of you. Chop-chop," Brad says.

271

I stumble into my room not very excited about whatever is going on, but willing to go with the flow. Between Friday night's disastrous double date with Reed and the chick that couldn't read the room, and then last night with Theo, I am beyond exhausted and just want to stay in bed today to mentally prepare for all the peopling I will be doing at the gala.

I look in the mirror and whisper my morning pep talk to myself, "Good morning, you beautiful bitch! Put some pep in your step so you can provide the pep for those who need it around you. Even though you did not sleep nearly enough, you look beautiful, you look healthy, and you look happy. You will conquer any fear that creeps into your life today." I pat my face with my hands to perk myself up a little more. "And if you fail at everything you have planned for today, you still have a man who loves you and will pick you up when you fall. Good talk, me." I smack my own ass and open the bedroom door to see what adventure awaits us this morning.

******

I am not horribly excited to see Reed when we pull up to where Brad is taking us. I sit back in the truck for a second after Brad and Avery get out for another quick mental pep talk. I don't need to go to jail today for beating up the douche who upset my best friend.

I walk up behind Sandy and loop my arm in hers. "So, knuckleheads, why did you drag us from our beauty sleep so early on a Sunday? Are we just going to stand here and chit chat or what?"

Brad gestures towards the boat. "Your chariot awaits, miladies."

I climb my way up with Brad's help and settle in on the seat next to him. I want to sit next to Sandy, but I know that I need to force her and Reed to be close enough to talk about whatever is going on with them. She has expressed how excited she is to be a private nanny and how this income will help her find her independence faster, so I need to step back to let that talk happen.

Brad hands me a coffee and a throw blanket, so I cover both of us up with it. I start talking with Brad quietly about some bands that will be playing soon in Orlando to make us seem unavailable to talk to so that Sandy or Reed will start the conversation they desperately need to have. When I see Sandy offer to share the blanket with Reed, I breathe a little easier and relax into silence for a few minutes.

"So, what are we doing out here, Gilligan?" I ask Brad.

"Give it a minute, Mrs. Howell, and you will see," Brad jokes.

After a few minutes of aimlessly looking around, I notice Reed positioning Sandy to look towards a spot in the water, so I follow where he is pointing.

"Ok, I have lived here for years and never knew that I could see this," I say softly.

Brad whispers, "I am surprised James hasn't brought you out here; he knows the spot."

I whisper back to him, "Well, we very rarely leave the bed much anymore, so I am not surprised that he hasn't."

Brad smirks. "That old man can still get it up? Impressive."

I smirk back at Brad. "He is extremely impressive."

The next hour is spent between small talk and moments of quiet self-reflection between us all. If I weren't already feeling anxious about tonight, this morning would have been the most serene experience I have ever had. I am zoned out the entire trip back to land and the entire walk back to the truck until Brad opens the door for me to get in. As I am pulling my seatbelt across my chest, Brad rolls down my window.

"Want to get dinner tonight when Lola gets home? That joint with the outdoor cornhole area she likes?"

Reed nods. "Yeah, I will see y'all there. Six work for everyone?"

"No can do, Buckaroo. I have work and Peach back here has a date tonight," I state.

"Be safe, Sandy. Hope you have a good date tonight. Brad, see you at six," Reed says,

Sandy leans her head between me and Brad. "Aves, tonight is not a date. Jayden left an open invitation to join him and his grandfather on any Sunday night. Besides, I don't know if I want to go. I think I should just stay home tonight and bake or something."

"Cookies," Brad says.

I smack Brad's arm. "Look, Peach, I know that the past couple of weeks have been emotional for you, and your life has done a complete 180 here, but I need my cowgirl back on her saddle. Even if I have to lock every pot, pan, and any other kitchen accessory away in my trunk for a bit. For too long you have not been put on the pedestal that belongs to you. I am not saying I want you to jump into a relationship or anything, but I do need you to remember that you are attractive, funny, and deserve to have men drool over you again. Your inner goddess has been snoozing too long, and we just need to wake and shake her up a bit. Go tonight. Flirt, dance, go with the flow, and fix your own crown because it keeps slipping every time you drop your face down. Just don't accept drinks from anyone, don't leave your drink with anyone, and don't take any shit from anyone."

Chapter 23
James

"Hey, Dad, how is everything going?"

"Hey, Jack! Everything is going pretty well down here. The new nanny is fitting in, Reed is happier, and Lola is acting more like she did before Betty left. Everything is really falling into place. How is work?"

"Same old, same old. Stackin' and rackin'. I have a lot of kids that come to my weekly story time, so that is fun and rewarding for the library side. The bartending, well, it's going. You know how dealing with inebriated hotheads goes."

I laugh. "Oh, I definitely do. Those years I did some part-time bartending when you were in high school to pay for your sports necessities was more than enough to make me loathe the bar scene. I do not envy you, Kid."

"It is what it is, I suppose. So, any updates on your lady friend? How is that going?"

I sigh. "It's going. I am not sure if we are stuck in a stagnant spot or if things will progress from where they are now, but I will let you know when I find out. I am letting her lead on this one."

"Sounds good, Dad. I have to run so I can find a parking spot at the bar for my shift. Get's pretty wild with playoffs. Love you, Dad."

"I love you, too, Jack. Be safe out there."

I hang up and glance around my living room. It is so empty on the nights that Avery doesn't come over. Tonight should have been my night, even though I am no longer a paying customer. But, she will be at the gala instead. I hope she will at least send me a picture of her all dressed up. I need to get out of here. I walk out to the golf cart. I still have some sunlight left, maybe I can find that damned hole in the fence.

I head to the main house to make a snack for my perimeter check. I have been awful at stocking my fridge since Betty left since I do most of the cooking at the main house now. Reed invited me to join him for dinner, but I opted out since I knew I was a little grumpy about not being able to see Avery tonight. It only made it worse that I didn't get to see her this entire weekend, but Brad did. I should have a talk with him about him butting into my limited time. I know he only looks at Avery as a friend, and I know he is a solid friend to have, but I need him to schedule his time around me and not vice versa until Avery and I can get back to a normal schedule of seeing each other. Pent-up sexual frustration is taking over my moods, I suppose.

"Hey, about to do your perimeter check?" Reed asks me.

I nod. "Yeah, I haven't found the hole yet, but I know there is one somewhere because I found a gator again the other day. They can't be getting through either gate without us seeing them when they are opened, so there has to be a hole in the fence somewhere."

"Want me to call the fencing company to come check it out? I can call them tomorrow?"

I shake my head. "No, I will find it eventually, and it is no added effort on my nightly checks."

Reed nods. "If you change your mind, let me know."

I raise my sandwich in the air in lieu of a wave and head back to the golf cart.

I drive up to the front gate and decide to start on the east side of the grounds tonight. With my shotgun beside me, I drive what I can and walk what I have to, checking the fence line. I won't be caught face to face with a gator alone with no way to protect myself if I need to.

About an hour later, the sun is starting to set, so I head back to my place with no hole found. I put my phone down on the kitchen counter while I take my shotgun to the gun safe I have in my room. I hear the phone ring a couple of times and then it stops, so I finish my task at hand. Because of Lola, Reed and I make it the highest priority to make sure all guns are safely locked up and out of her reach at all times. I was the same way about gun safety with Jack.

As I enter the kitchen, my phone rings again.

"Hey boss, what's up?" I ask when I answer.

"I need you to get here, and fast. I have to go pick up Sandy," Reed rushes out.

"On my way," I say before hanging up and running back out to the golf cart.

******

When Reed called me to tell me to call Peter, I waste no time in reaching out to him.

"Hey, Doc, can you come over to the main house?" I ask him.

"You know, James, if you are trying to sweep Ms. Avery off her feet, you should do it the old-fashioned way so we don't risk concussions so many times," Peter jokes.

I sigh. "I wish it were for Avery instead. Our nanny was out at a bar and called for help. Reed thinks she was drugged and went to get her."

I hear rustling on the other end of the line. "On my way, James. Be there in just a few minutes."

I run my fingers through my hair. "Thanks, Doc, the front door is unlocked for you."

****

I am pacing the garage when Reed finally pulls up. "Doc is in the living room."

I help get Sandy out and settled into Reed's arms. Looking at her so helpless and out of it has my stomach in knots. Not only am I concerned about Sandy and her safety, but it also makes me think of Avery and what I would do if it were her in this situation. I am pacing the kitchen listening to Reed and Peter talk back and forth, but not registering what they are saying. My mind keeps drifting to Avery. I need to call her.

The ride from the house to Peter's to drop him off is silent until I park the golf cart.

"She is Avery's best friend. What should I tell Avery?" I ask Peter.

He places a hand on my shoulder. "That she will need her friend, but we won't know more until the bloodwork comes back and Sandy has a kit done. For now, that is all the advice I can give."

I nod my head and watch Peter make his way into his house. I sit there for a minute just staring at my phone before finally making the call. It rings twice and then goes to voicemail. I know she is at the gala, but this is important, so I call again. It rings three times and then goes to voicemail.

"Fuck, Dove, answer your damn phone. Please. Call me immediately."

I drive back towards the main house, and when I walk in, I find Sandy and Reed are no longer in the living room. I sit down on the couch and try calling Avery again.

"The person you are trying to reach is unavailable…"

"What the fuck?" I whisper while staring at my phone. Did she block my call? I lean back on the couch and figure out a game plan for what to do. First and foremost, I am needed here; Reed will have his hands full taking care of Sandy, so I can't just go camp outside Avery's house until she gets home. I'll call Brad; he can camp out.

"What could be going on that you would decide I am worthy of a phone call from you this late on a Sunday night?" Brad asks.

"Not time for the jokes, Brad. Sandy was drugged tonight. She is here with us and safe, but I can't get a hold of Avery," I rush out.

"I told that fucking dimwit to make up some nanny emergency to stop her from going to that fucking bar tonight! I just knew this was going to happen. If I see that blond Don Juan, he will be eating my fists," Brad starts ranting. "One day Reed will actually listen to me. Okay. Let me try calling her really quick."

Brad hangs up, and within a minute, he is calling me back. "Dude, I think she blocked me."

I rub a hand down my face. "Yeah, I think she blocked me, too."

Brad sighs out, "Alright, I will watch for her car. As soon as I see her, I will haul ass over there and then call you. Keep your phone near you. What can I do to help Sandy and Reed?"

I tap my fingers on the coffee table. "Nothing really. They are resting now; I'm going to stay at the main house and take care of Lola. I will keep my phone on me. Thanks for helping. You being so close to her house is actually the best help we can have right now. Talk to you when you catch her."

"Yeah, man, no problem. Let me know if y'all need anything else from me."

The line goes dead, and I sit there just staring at the table in front of me. I need to get some rest, but I know that sleep won't come easily for me tonight. Not only because of concern for what happened with Sandy, but with why I can't get a hold of Avery. Why would she block not only my calls but Brad's as well? It doesn't make any sense.

Chapter 24
Avery

I am walking around the event center looking for Cal after my quick bathroom break turned into a twenty-five-minute ordeal. You would think that the people running this place would have more than six women's stalls for an event room that holds hundreds of people. Had I known that there would be a long wait, I would have at least brought my phone so I could check in with Sandy and see how her "not date" is going.

"Avie Baby, there you are," Cal says as he wraps an arm around my waist.

I don't know when he decided that we should have nicknames, but he has decided that 'Avie Baby' is my name for tonight. "Oh, finally! I have been walking around trying to find you. Sorry I was gone so long."

Cal hands me my handbag. "I was about to call for search and rescue, but heard a couple of women complaining about the wait for the bathroom being longer than the wait at the bar."

I huff out a laugh. "You have no idea!" I reach into my purse to check my phone. Hitting the side button, I don't see any missed texts or calls. I suppose Sandy's night is going well, then. "Do we have many more elbows to rub, or are we close to calling it a night? It is nearly midnight, and we still have an hour drive home."

Cal shrugs. "I have a few more to rub against, and we can head out. I can get us a room down the road if you want. We have both been drinking, so driving, doesn't sound like a good idea."

I put a hand on Cal's. "I thought you said you quit drinking like two hours ago so that you could get us home safely. Did you not?" I ask.

Cal runs a hand through his hair. "Well, I did, but when you were in the bathroom, one of the top investors at our hospital came over to me with a glass of bourbon. I couldn't turn it down, and one turned into three while waiting on you."

I look to the ground for a second and then raise my head to his. "Well, that is unfortunate, but I quit drinking about an hour ago and only had two glasses of champagne for the night. I should be more than sober enough to drive us home."

Cal shakes his head. "Sorry, Avie Baby. Even though I believe you are 'sober enough' to drive, I don't believe you are sober enough to drive my Camero. That car is my baby. We can just get a room; it's no big deal. I promise."

I narrow my eyes at him. "No, it is a big deal. I did not agree to sharing a hotel room with you tonight, nor did

I agree to staying in Orlando for the night. I have to get home, even if that means getting a ride from someone else."

I go to pull away from Cal's arm around me, but he tightens his hold. "Don't be dramatic, Avie Baby. Come on." He runs a finger down my cheek. "Let's just get a room for the night."

I jerk out of his grip. "Goodnight, Cal."

I start walking towards the door but hear Cal calling behind me so I swerve and head to the women's restroom again. I sneak to the front of the line and whisper yell at the ladies gawking at me, "I don't need the facilities, just need to hide."

The women all start looking around and shoo me into the bathroom. I pull out my phone and search for my Uber app that I haven't needed in months.

"Don't mind me," I whisper at the women who I startle from my hiding spot behind the door. "I'm just hiding from my overly handsy date who isn't getting the hint. I promise I am not a creepy weirdo."

I can hear Cal outside the bathroom and every woman leaving telling him that there is no one in a purple dress in here. A woman pops her head in a few minutes later to let me know that the coast is clear to leave my hiding spot. With a sincere, gratuitous hug, I leave the bathroom and sprint for the front door where my Uber is waiting for me.

******

An hour later, I am waving goodbye to my new friend Donnie, the Uber driver. "You do not let her make you feel that way, Don Don! You are a good soul and if you are too much for her, tell her to go find less!"

"Avery! Thank you for the talk! If you ever need a ride again, find me on the app; I always leave it on. Be safe, butterfly!"

I flap my pretend wings and turn with a smile to head into my house. I am startled by Brad relaxing on my porch swing.

"Butterfly?" he asks quietly.

"Yes, butterfly. I sang Mariah with my new friend, Don Don. If I was shelling out that kind of money for an Uber all the way back home, I was going to get my money's worth and demanded a mini-Mariah concert. Don Don obliged me," I say, thumb hitched over my shoulder.

Brad leans forward and put his elbows on his knees. "I am so glad that you had such a fun night that you decided neither myself nor James were worthy of you answering our phone calls."

"What are you talking about? I never got a call from either of you," I say, fishing my phone out of my bag.

Before I can pull my phone out, Brad turns his screen to show me the nineteen times he tried calling me over the last two and a half hours.

I flip my phone around to show him my screen. "See, I have nothing."

Brad grabs my phone, opens his contact information and points to the option that says, "unblock caller."

"What the fuck?" I whisper out. "I swear I didn't block you!"

Brad nods his head wearily. "Well, fix James's while you are at it. Crazy that you didn't block us, but the one night we both needed to get a hold of you, we couldn't."

"What did you two need?" I ask while switching over to James's contact information to unblock him as well.

"Sandy was drugged," Brad says flatly.

I whip my head up. "What? Where is she? Is she okay?"

Brad raises his hands. "She is okay. She is with Reed. She couldn't get through to you or James, so she called Reed. James called me when he couldn't get in touch with you, and then Reed called me shortly after to let me know what happened. Reed's neighbor is a doctor and checked her out. He said rest is all that will help right now."

I unlock my door and rush inside. I need to get out of this dress; it is making me feel claustrophobic. "Unzip me, Brad! Hurry!" I yell at him. "Get me out of this fucking thing!"

Brad unzips the back of my dress. "Calm down, Avery. Breathe. She is okay. I heard it from James and Reed."

I shake my head and step out of my dress, not even caring that Brad is seeing my bare breasts- since I couldn't wear a bra with that dress- and my thong-clad ass to avoid panty lines. I power walk to my room and rummage around for a pair of sweats.

"I knew that something happened to Talia, and I still let Sandy meet up with that guy alone! I am the worst friend in the world! Brad! I am so awful," I cry out.

Brad wraps his big arms around me. "You are not to blame, Avey Davey, you are not to blame for what happened tonight at all! It could happen to anyone and has in the past. You couldn't have known that this would happen to her. Sit down, I am going to call James and let him know that I am here with you."

I nod my head and lower myself onto my bed. Pulling my legs up to my chest, I get lost in my own head for a bit until I feel the bed shift beside me.

"Alright, Davey, what happened tonight? Let's start from the beginning."

I throw a sweatshirt over my head and turn to face Brad. "I am not a bartender. I am a professional cuddler. Tonight, I swayed from the normal visit with a regular client of mine. He asked me to go to a work thing with him; I agreed because he has been a client for a long while and has always been very respectful. I think he purposefully drank more than intended and then tried to convince me to stay in

Orlando with him. He had my phone and purse around the time that you and James were trying to get in touch with me. I could never imagine him blocking your numbers, but I also could never imagine that he would have been as forward as he was tonight. I hid in a bathroom until my Uber arrived and then came home. That is all of it in a nutshell."

Brad nods. "Does James know about this job and this guy?"

I stare blankly at Brad.

"So, he knows about one of them or both?"

"Both, to an extent. He knows of my job, and he knows where I was tonight and why. He just doesn't know the who. No one can know the who, that is part of my terms, that confidentiality is upheld."

Brad shakes his head. "Does the guy tonight deserve that confidentiality still?"

I bite my lip before responding, "For now, yes. While he was forward, he didn't get a chance to cross any uncrossable boundaries. And who knows, maybe I jumped the gun and his offer to get a room was still strictly platonic. I don't know, I didn't give him a chance to prove anything one way or the other."

Brad shakes his head. "Do not ever second-guess your gut instinct! Do you hear me?"

I nod.

Brad grabs my hands. "Alright, put some pants on. I'll make you some food, or tea, or whatever you need right now. I am staying with you for the rest of the night per James's request. He wanted me to let you know that he wishes he could be the one here with you, but he is staying at the house for Lola and Sandy."

I nod my head. "Thank you. Some tea sounds good, but I will make it."

Brad puts a hand on my shoulder. "No ma'am. You drank my coffee, and you ate at a restaurant with me. Don't backslide now. James told me since you and I spend so much time together. You know you are safe with me."

"I don't know if I love you or hate you, but you are right. Thank you. Not only for tonight but for being my push buddy- even when I push back," I say as I lean back in my bed.

Lucy Fur finally emerges from her favorite spot under my bed and cuddles on my lap for her pets. When Brad comes back in with my tea, he lays on the opposite end of my bed and tells me stories of his life until I fall asleep.

******

By noon, I am blowing up Sandy's phone with text messages. I have tried calling James twice, but he hasn't answered my calls. Brad already left for work and being alone right now has me on edge. Lucy has been an awful companion through all of this; she just keeps meowing and then running back under the bed. Little hussy won't even keep me company to slow down my overactive imagination.

When my phone rings, I jump to grab it from the other side of the couch where I threw it twenty minutes ago.

"Oh my God, Peach! What happened? Reed told Brad, and Brad told me. Do I need to come whoop Reed's ass? Is he making you work right now? I can be there in about twelve minutes if I speed."

I can hear the sadness in Sandy's voice when she whispers, "I need to go have a kit done. I need you with me."

"I'll be there, Peach."

******

I find Reed's truck easily enough at the hospital and park close to him. I walk over to his passenger door and put my arm around Sandy when she gets out of the truck. My body is on autopilot as we walk into the hospital; Sandy talks to the nurse and then she and I are escorted to the back. Neither one of us says a word while the nurse and doctor explain the exam process and what they need Sandy to do. It is like the world is moving around us in slow motion until the doctor finally pulls her gloves off.

"I do have some good news: From my exam, I don't see any signs of trauma. In my medical opinion, you were not physically assaulted after being drugged last night. To be on the safe side, I am still going to prescribe some medicine to take to prevent any infections," the doctor says to Sandy.

A mix between a gasp and a sob rip through Sandy's lips and I rush over to throw my arms around her. I am holding her so tight that I am afraid I might bruise her, but the way she is gripping me closer tells me that she needs this tight hug right now.

When we walk back into the waiting area to find Reed, I drop my hand from Sandy's as soon as she and

Reed lock eyes. He rushes over to her and wraps her in a hug and I watch as she falls into his embrace. I feel selfish right now because even with everything that Sandy just went through, I am jealous that she has Reed for comfort right now. I need James. I need his comfort but he still has not returned my calls.

I walk out of the hospital with them and let Reed know that I will be taking Sandy home with me. I wait while he embraces her again, and then we head to my Jeep.

"Do you want anything from anywhere on the way home? I figured I would drop you off and then go get your medicines so you can shower in peace."

Sandy shakes her head. "I can't think of anything I need. I am just ready to shower and relax."

I nod. "Understandable. You earned a sympathy card; tonight's movie is your choice."

Sandy giggles. "I haven't earned a sympathy card in seventeen years. I don't know if I am sad or happy to receive this one."

I shrug my shoulders. "You know I am stingy with my sympathy cards, take the win while you can."

Sandy smiles at me. "You are the best, except when you are singing."

I lightly smack Sandy's leg. "You are walking a fine line there, Peach. A mighty fine line."

Sandy grabs my hand. "I tried calling you last night."

I squeeze her hand back. "I know, I will tell you all about it tonight. Needless to say, I am dropping two shifts a week."

Chapter 25
James

Now that Reed is home, I can call Avery back. I didn't want to answer her call when I had Lola because I needed to make sure we could speak openly. With the time I have had to think about everything, I feel like a phone conversation won't cut it. Once I am settled between my sheets, I call her.

"Hey," she says quietly.

"Hi," I say flatly.

"I am sorry," she starts.

"I am off tomorrow morning. Why don't we meet at our spot to have this conversation?"

Avery sighs. "Whatever you want to do, I guess. I truly am sorry."

I know I sound like an asshole, but I am still not over what happened. "Yeah, we can talk about it tomorrow. See you at nine."

Before she can respond, I hang up. I need to mentally prepare myself for the talk we will have in the morning. It is long overdue at this point.

******

I am sitting at our table when Avery walks in. For the first time on one of our coffee dates, I do not stand to greet her. She walks up beside me, bends down, and kisses my head, then sits across from me. I slide the coffee I got for her across the table before finally looking up and looking into her eyes.

She wraps both of her hands around her coffee and leans across the table to be closer to me. "James, I am so extremely sorry about the phone incident. I promise you that I did not block you. I know who did and it is my own fault for asking him to hold my purse and phone while I ran to the bathroom."

I nod. "Who was it?" I ask.

Avery solemnly shakes her head. "You know I can't answer that, James."

I cock my head to the side. "Can't or just won't? Because from where I am sitting, this guy lost the right to anonymity when he went through your personal phone and blocked your boyfriend. The fact that it was an emergency situation only amplifies my right to know."

Avery's eyes narrow at me. "First things first: I am not your girlfriend. You do not own the rights to me or my secrets. Second, I have handled the situation and informed the gentleman that he is no longer a client of mine."

I shake my head in disbelief. "You are right, Dove. You are not my girlfriend. You have made it abundantly clear that you do not want that title, yet I have been the dumbass who was willing to settle for what little scraps you gave me time and time again."

Avery jerks up and pulls her shoulders back. "Scraps? Was my virginity scraps, James?"

"No, Dove. Your virginity was not, but your time and access to your life has been just that. I got what was left after your business, but it was conditional around your work. Those are the scraps I received. This was a mistake. I should leave."

I stand to leave, but Avery stops me. "Please don't leave. I am sorry. I'm being defensive. Let's start this morning over."

I slowly sit back down.

"Can we go to your place to talk? I really am not okay. Since Sunday, all I wanted to do was to snuggle up into your arms and feel safe again."

I can see Avery's lip trembling. I stand and pull her up into a hug. "Come on, Dove, let's go to my place and I will give you my mending cuddles this time."

Avery lets out a mix between a sob and a laugh. "Thank you."

******

After dropping her Jeep off at her house, we made our way to my place. I got a text from Reed telling me to take the whole day off instead of just the morning, and that he was taking Sandy and Lola out for a day trip around Orlando. Once inside, I grab Avery's hand and lead her to the kitchen.

"I haven't eaten breakfast yet, so I am going to make some pancakes while you tell me what happened," I state.

Avery shrugs. "Fair enough. Make some for me, too."

I eye her suspiciously. "Who are you and what have you done with the real Avery?"

She rolls her eyes. "Shut up and start cooking. And while you do not agree with it, I am still going to keep some anonymity for my former client. So for conversations sake, I will be calling him 'Prick.' "

I chuckle, "For now, I will allow this."

Avery rolls her shoulders back and then jumps up on the counter next to the stove. "So, I already didn't want to be there. I knew that long before I even showed up at his house yesterday. I wanted to cancel and come here but felt like that would be shitty business practice for me, so I went.

The night started off fine; typically polite conversations, I found one bartender and would watch his champagne bottles. I had two glasses and made sure that I got the first pour from a freshly opened bottle and that no one else was able to be near my drink. The rest of the time, I had bottled water. Anyway, Prick was schmoozing and cruising through the sea of investors. When we made our way near the bathrooms, I decided to take advantage of the proximity and handed my purse over to him- which had my phone inside of it. I did not realize that I would be in a nearly thirty minutes long 'hold my pee' line. I plan to email the event center to let them know that only having six women's stalls open for an event that large is absurd.

Anyway, when I found Prick again, he said we were almost done there and kept insisting on renting a hotel room."

I abandon the pancake batter I am mixing and put my hands on the counter on either side of Avery. Dropping my head into her lap, I mutter against her legs, "I don't know if I can hear any more of this, Dove, but I know that I need to."

Avery runs her hand through my hair. "I am almost past this part. So, I offered to drive us home, he said no, so

I got an Uber. I had a very polite and respectful driver. When I got home, Brad was waiting on my porch swing."

I lift my head and go back to the pancakes. "Okay, so what? The prick blocked me?"

Avery nods. "That is the only conclusion that I can think of. I checked the times that Brad tried calling me, and it lined up with when I was in the bathroom. I only know because I checked my phone after I got it back to see if Sandy had messaged or called me. I was curious to see how her 'not date' was going."

I step up to the heated pan at the stove. "Obviously not well."

Avery nods her head slowly. "Yeah, can you tell me what you know about that?"

I slap some butter in the pan. "I got a call from Reed to come watch Lola so he could go get Sandy. She tried calling me when she couldn't reach you, but I was away from my phone. When he got back from picking her up…." I shake my head remembering the way Sandy looked in Reed's arms. "It was hard to see. She was in and out of consciousness, murmuring incoherent words here and there. If it weren't for me seeing her chest move up and down with her breaths, there are times that I wouldn't have believed she was even alive. It was very scary and I am glad you weren't here to witness it, honestly."

Avery sniffles. "I am thankful that she had you and Reed here to take care of her. Thank you for that."

I reach over and dry Avery's tears. "I love you, Dove. She is your best friend, so I will always watch over and protect her in the same way that I will for you. Always."

Avery nuzzles her head against my hand. "I had a small anxiety attack when I got home, and Brad told me what happened. He saw me nearly naked. Please don't be mad. It wasn't anything sexual. I started panicking, and my dress was freaking me out and I felt stuck. He unzipped it for me and I just dropped it to the floor. I felt like it was suffocating me."

I rub her cheek with my thumb. "Brad already told me. I am not mad. I did threaten to gouge his eyes out with a gardening shovel if I ever thought he added that image to his spank bank, though."

Avery lets out a soft laugh. "For his sake, I hope he doesn't. I think that with what happened with Prick and then finding out about what happened to Sandy, it put me in a really weird, nearly PTSD mindset. I felt very numb, but not by choice. Like my mind had to shut down for a few minutes to survive. I don't know. But I do know that the entire time, all that I could hold on to was thoughts of you and how I wanted, or maybe needed, you to pull me out of it."

"I can see how the night's events could trigger something like that."

Avery drops her head and sniffles again. "I don't want to lose you, James. I love you and I really want you in my life."

I take the last pancake off the pan and set it aside. "Dove, I love you too, and I really want to be in your life. Let's eat and we can continue this after we have full bellies."

******

Talking after brunch led to cuddling, which led to an impromptu nap. Waking up with Avery in my arms again reminds me of how good we have had it, but also all of the bumps in the road. This bed is where we started our journey nearly a year ago. I run my arm along her side and she pushes her ass back into my growing erection.

"Dove, I don't think we should do this just yet," I whisper to her.

She backs her ass up against me again. "I need this connection between us. Please?"

I am battling an inner demon right now. I want to give her what she wants and thinks she needs, but the other part of me knows that this is a bad idea because we have not worked through our problems yet. While we talked about what happened on Sunday, we did not fix anything, nor did we even scratch the surface of the root cause of our issues.

Avery rolls over, pushing me to my back and then mounts herself on me.

I grab either side of her hips. "Avery…"

She leans down, her kiss against my lips is desperate. "Please?"

I tighten my grip and shake my head. "I can't. Mahout."

Avery's head snaps back, and she jumps off of me. "Can you take me home, please?"

I sit up. "Avery, we need to talk more."

"Just take me home."

I watch as Avery crosses her arms over her chest, effectively closing herself off from me. I roll out of bed knowing that anything I say right now will only make things worse. I drop my head and dread every step through my house to my car. The drive to her house is awkwardly silent, the air heavy. I can feel in my heart that this is the end of us. Not by my choice but by her pride.

When we pull up to her house, I turn to try to talk to her, but she throws open the passenger door and runs inside. I rub my hands over my face before hitting my steering wheel. I glance over towards Brad's but see the neighbor between Brad and Avery's house staring at me along with his funny-looking dog. I give a polite wave and back out of the driveway. I just need to give Avery some space for now. Everything is still fresh and emotions are running high. I will try to reach out in a couple of days when we get back from Illinois.

Chapter 26
Avery

"The absolute nerve of him! Who does he think he is, turning me down like that? Lucy! Are you even paying attention?" I look down at the floor to see that Lucy has retreated under my bed again. "The absolute nerve of you, too! I guess I need to wait for Sandy to get home before I can vent... screw this. I'm going to the store to get some rum. Do you want anything?" I look back and wait for Lucy Fur to give any sign that she is listening, but get nothing from her. "Lucy Elizabeth Fur, you are grounded. I am tired of your disrespect. Just because you are a teen, does not mean you get to get away with this."

I grab my keys and jump into my Jeep to hit the store a couple of blocks away. I will grab some food for dinner and a bottle of rum to drown my sorrows. I wish I could talk to Sandy about what happened today, but I can't for multiple reasons. One, I have kept him a secret and now that it is over, there is no point in bringing our hidden relationship to light. Second, he is a former client and I will still uphold my anonymity rules for him, even if he finds them ridiculous. I could talk to Brad about it all, but I don't want to risk my private thoughts getting back to James. That leaves rum. I need a rum bottle to hold my secrets for a bit.

Walking through the grocery store, I take my time checking out the meat and veggie selection trying to figure out what sounds good for dinner. I turn to make my way back to the zucchini when a hand reaches out and touches my arm.

"Avery, I am so glad I ran into you! I need to talk to you and I didn't want to have this conversation through email."

I roll my eyes. "Cal, of all the people I had hoped to see today, you didn't even make my list. Excuse me, you have caused enough problems in my life."

"Avery, please, I am so unbelievably sorry," he whispers. "I realized after you ran from me that the way I said what I said came off wrong. I truly was only trying to keep us safe and wanted to get us separate rooms."

I scoff and continue walking through the grocery store. "Yeah, whatever you say, Cal."

"Avery, you have to believe me. Please, I never meant to disrespect you. And the comment about my car, I don't let anyone drive it- not even Callie. My best friend and I restored it in high school. Toby and I worked on it for an entire year. After Toby passed, I have never let anyone else drive it or work on it. I didn't say it to be rude, I promise you."

I stop and look into Cal's eyes. "And blocking two guys in my phone was an accident, too?"

Cal whips his head back. "What are you talking about? I never touched your phone." Cal runs his hand down his face. "Wait, when I was talking to," Cal pauses, snapping his fingers. "Oh, what was his damn name? Charlie? Chuck?"

I roll my hand in the air. "Semantics, Cal…"

Cal pinches the bridge of his nose. "Yeah. Anyway, when I was talking to him, his girlfriend seemed a little drunk. She fell and when I tried to grab her, I dropped your purse and your phone fell out. I thought I put yours back in your purse, but a few minutes later, his girlfriend, Jennifer, Jenna, or whatever, came back and handed me yours. I had accidentally put her phone in your purse. I swear to you that I would never betray your trust by going through your phone."

I nod in acknowledgment. "I am really not in the headspace to talk about all of this right now. I truly just want to get my dinner and go home. Send me your availability for this weekend and we can meet up to chat somewhere."

Cal grabs and squeezes my hand. "Sounds like a plan. I really am sorry for upsetting you and messing everything up. I will email you with a time frame. See you later, Avery."

I give Cal a polite wave and continue to wander down the aisle that I don't even need to be on. Why is this my life right now? I need a break. Maybe I should plan a getaway for myself.

******

I am sitting at the closed lifeguard stand waiting for Cal and watching the waves break along the shore. I nearly forgot how beautiful the beach can be at night. I am not particularly happy that I had to wait until the sun fell to meet up with him, but I know his work schedule can be chaotic.

When he walks up to find me with my feet dangling over the edge leaning against the rail, he sits down beside me in the same manner.

"Do I have a chance of redeeming your view of me?" he asks quietly into the night.

I look in the opposite direction of him. "If you didn't, I wouldn't be here."

"Fair enough."

I look at him. "Redeem yourself."

Cal nods his head. "Let me start by telling you about Toby. Toby and I grew up on the same street, he was my best friend for my entire life. We spent every single day together. We planned to leave here and go to college in Louisiana, Toby wanted to play baseball for LSU. He was the athlete and I was the nerdy valedictorian. Nobody understood how we could be so different but still be best friends.

From eighth grade to junior year, we mowed lawns and did landscaping for all of our parents' friends and neighbors, saving every penny for our dream car."

"A 1960s Camero," I whisper.

Cal nods. "1968 SS. We found one in rough condition. We spent an entire year working at the skating rink while still doing yard work to afford the parts we needed to get it running. We read books, found a shop that would let us stand back to observe and would teach us what we needed to do to get our car up and running.

One night, we decided to go park where all the other guys with macho cars would park on Friday nights. We were mingling around and when we got back to the car, it wouldn't start. I popped open the hood and Toby was tinkering around with a cable. Some guy a couple of cars over honked his horn causing Toby to jerk back and hit his head on the hood. He did get the car running again a few minutes later."

Cal looks down at his lap and I can see tears stains appearing on his shorts. "A day and a half later, I got a call that Toby had died in his sleep. His parents had left for a weekend trip and came home to find him in his bed that Sunday afternoon. The autopsy showed he had died from an intracranial hemorrhage. I knew that he kept saying Saturday that he was tired and just not feeling great. It was nothing new for him to feel that way on Saturdays after having baseball practice in the mornings, so I just figured he was exhausted from that. Sunday, when he didn't come over for breakfast like usual, I assumed he still just didn't feel good. I should have gone over to his house to check on him."

I rub my hands across Cal's shoulders. "You were a kid still, you couldn't have known."

Cal wipes his cheeks. "I know that now."

"Is that why you went into medicine?" I ask.

Cal nods. "Yeah, and it is why when you didn't have someone to sit with you after your accident, I went with you."

I can't stop the soft sob that breaks from my lips. "Cal, oh, I am so sorry."

Cal looks up at me. "Toby wasn't just my friend, Avery. He was my boyfriend. My soulmate. He was it for me."

I throw my arms around Cal and pull him into the tightest hug I can manage. There is nothing that I can say in this moment to ease his grief of trudging through all of this again.

Cal sniffles. "I am a gay man. I have known this for years, but I haven't come out of the closet. Callie has known since Toby died, and now you. I didn't see the point in telling anyone because I will never find someone who could fill the shoes that Toby left behind. Your easy-going vibe reminds me of him. Please do not hate me, but when you cuddle me, I imagine that it is him holding me. At the gala, I was pushy because I felt like I had to put on a show to fit in with the other men there. I saw the way they all looked at you, so I felt like I needed to do more to stay hidden in my closet."

I shake my head. "Cal, your secret is safe with me and I will never be mad at you for finding comfort in my arms, even if it isn't my arms you are imagining. I cannot even fathom the pain you have gone through; how you faced that grief mostly alone. I am here for you, as your friend, always."

Cal turns to me and hugs me. "Will you allow me to be a client again? I still could use some of your 'magical mending cuddles' and I swear to you that I will never put on my straight façade around you ever again."

I nod against his neck. "Of course." I pull my head back. "It all makes sense now."

Cal cocks his head to the side. "What does?"

I laugh out, "Why you are so good at picking out dresses and nighties with the fabulous robes."

Cal drops his head with a laugh. "Yeah, like I said, Toby wanted to play for LSU and purple was one of his two favorite colors. I guess old habits die hard and whether it's a t-shirt or lingerie, I tend to lean toward purples. He would have loved you. He always told me that he hoped that someday we would have our best girlfriend who would hang out with us for games and drinks."

I grab both of Cal's hands in mine. "I think we should go play a round of Rummy with a cocktail for Toby."

Cal nods. Standing up, he grabs my hand and pulls me to stand beside him. "Thank you for sticking around while I am battling my inner demons, or grieving them, I suppose."

Cal's words make me pause and my heart squeeze. I remember my first encounter with James, *"Um, thank you, I promise I am okay. Battling inner demons, and I forgot my holy water in my other purse."* He laughed and said, *"I see, would you like company so you aren't battling alone?"* This week has been full of me going over every millisecond of the last two weeks with and without him. I have debated calling him multiple times, but don't want to bother him while he is on his business trip. I will make it a point to see him when they get back in a couple of days.

Chapter 27
James

The flight home from Illinois reminds me of the return flight from the last business trip: Me "simpering," as Jack would put it, for Avery while having no communication from her. At least this time, I knew the reasoning behind the no-contact situation. The text I sent last night asking her if we could meet to talk today was answered this morning with a simple, "Yes," with a coffee cup emoji. I have an hour left of the flight and then another hour drive to figure out how I am going to tell her that I went on a date while I was gone.

******

When I get to our coffee shop, Avery is waiting for me at a different table than normal with only one coffee in front of her. I walk up to the barista and place my order before glancing at Avery. She is watching me with a smile. I am so confused right now.

I grab my coffee from the barista and walk to the table. "Avery, I…."

Avery puts her hands up. "Please, let me go first."

I sit down and wave my hand in front of me to encourage her to speak.

Avery fidgets with her fingers. "While you were gone, I did a lot of self-reflecting. I was completely out of line the other day, and you were right to stop us from… uhh, well, stop us from continuing what I was trying to start. I did not respect your concerns and I am very sorry about that. I had a talk with my former client and learned that a lot of what happened the night of the gala was a gigantic series of misunderstandings and unfortunate accidents."

I look down at my coffee but nod my head to let her know that I am still receptive to what she is saying.

Avery clears her throat. "And to be transparent with you, I have brought him back on as a client."

My eyes meet hers and I bite my bottom lip to stop myself from saying anything. I told her I would let her go first, and I will keep my word.

Avery looks down at her hands. "I know that this will be a point of contention with you, but I want to lay all of our cards out on the table and start fresh with each other."

"Is that all?" I ask

Avery nods. "For now."

I lean forward and brace my arms on the table. "I do not have a say in who or what you do with your business. I am not your boyfriend, not by my choice, but I have respected yours. To lay all of my cards on the table and start fresh with each other, as you put it, I went on a date while I was away."

Avery scoots her chair back and crosses her arms across her chest. "Are you fucking serious?" She whispers.

I straighten in my seat. "I am fucking serious. Like I said, I am not your boyfriend, but not by my choice. I did some self-reflecting as well, Avery. I realized that I put my love life on the back burner for years to make being a father my first priority. I didn't date because I didn't want someone else that Jack would have to lose or watch walk away. Once Jack left for college, dating never crossed my mind until you came into my life. You made me realize what I was missing. With that being said, I will not put my dating life on hold any longer."

"So what? You just fell out of love with me that easily?" She asks, tears filling her eyes.

"God no, Avery. I love you so much it hurts. But it only hurts because you can't give me what I need. I can't keep being the guy you turn to for sex and companionship with no relationship. I can't keep going to bed at night while you are in someone else's bed; even though I do trust that it is strictly work and nothing more. I just can't do it anymore."

Avery looks everywhere but at me. "So, we are just done?"

I shrug solemnly. "That is your choice, Avery. I hate to leave you with an ultimatum, but it is all I can do now. I will respect whichever you choose. It will either be me as your boyfriend and you find a new job, or we can call it quits and be friends. We have been seeing each other for a year; we have taken our time, but I can't do the partial love anymore."

Avery stands and extends a hand to me. "It was nice doing business with you, Mr. Sullivan. You have my email address. If you ever feel my services are needed again, just reach out. I will try to fit you in where I can."

I look at Avery's extended hand but can't bring myself to shake it. I know that I gave the ultimatum, but I really thought that she would choose me. I told her I would respect her decision, though, so with hesitation, I grab her hand to shake it. "Thank you, Ms. Jones."

I sit back down and watch Avery walk out of the coffee shop, head held high and shoulders straight. Finally looking like the queen I always told her she was.

******

"Dad? Are you there?"

I snap out of my haze. "Sorry, Jack, what did you say?"

"I was saying that this semester will be a little lighter for me from the looks of it. I know it's a few months away, but I was thinking I would come visit for Thanksgiving if that works for you?"

I look at the calendar by my fridge, not believing that it's already August. "Of course, Kid, I would love that! You can take my room and I will stay up at the main house so you can still have some privacy.

"I can crash on the couch, Dad. I am coming to see you and I actually want to be around you. You should be thankful for that. Most everyone I know hates being around their parents."

"I am very thankful! You just tell me the dates and how you want to travel here. I can buy your plane tickets, or if you want to drive, I will rent you a car so you aren't driving that death trap on wheels you love so much."

"If you ever rode a motorcycle, you would find that it is not as terrifying as you think. How about I give you a few lessons while I am there?"

"Dream on, Kiddo, I am too old to learn new tricks," I laugh out.

"You are only as old as you feel, Dad. I have to run, bar shift tonight. I love you!"

"I love you, too, Jack. Talk again soon." I pull the phone away from my ear and hang up.

I wonder if Avery ever exchanged that plane ticket I bought her since she doesn't need to go to Texas to see Sandy. Maybe she will go visit her parents. It has been eight weeks since I lost her in our coffee shop. Eight weeks of missing her and wishing I would have never given her that ultimatum. Eight weeks of kicking myself in the ass for believing I could handle being on the back burner even though I know I deserve to be put first in a relationship.

Dottie will be in town next week. I am glad I exchanged numbers with her in Chicago, even though it made me sick at the time. She has become a close friend and with the time she will be spending here for work, maybe there could be more there someday.

We have a lot in common; she is also in her early forties with an adult child. She travels for work as a nurse since her son went off to college. She is a widow who never looked for love or worried about dating. I was her first date in a decade when we met at the hotel bar in Chicago. She is beautiful in a traditional manner: shoulder-length light brown hair with blonde thrown in, slender, average height, crow's feet around her eyes and laugh lines around her mouth showing that her forty-something years have been happy ones.

We have a date planned for the night that she arrives. I plan to take her to this British themed pub for drinks. She mentioned that she loves every show on the BBC app, so I thought I would surprise her with this fun place.

******

Pulling up to the pub, I get out of my car and walk to the passenger side to let Dottie out. She grabs my extended hand, pulls herself out of the car, and then straightens her dress.

"Are you sure I am not overdressed?" She asks me.

I back away a step and look down at her outfit.

"You look beautiful. I believe we are both overdressed and

probably pushing the age limit for who they allow in, but I think we can manage it regardless."

Dottie giggles. "You sure know how to make a woman feel special," she says before standing on her tip toes to kiss my cheek and pat my chest.

I put my hand on the small of her back to lead her inside. "Oh, if you think this is good now, it only gets better with alcohol. My sexy slurring with the one eye focusing will really get you going."

She lets out a loud laugh. "I can't wait to see this."

Chapter 28
Avery

It took me weeks to muster up the nerve to ask Sandy if she would spend a weekend with her pathetic roommate rather than her sexy boyfriend, just to pull up to the bar on our first girls' night in weeks and see the man I have been avoiding with another woman. I sat there and watched as she threw her head back to laugh at whatever he said, watched her pat his chest and kiss his cheek. Those laughs, that chest, and that cheek used to be mine. I want to instantly hate her, but I can't because I know that losing him was my own fault. I am glad to see him laughing and happy.

"Ok, Aves, let's shake our asses and tip some glasses," Sandy says after checking her lip gloss.

I snap out of my pity party for one. "In the words of our country queen, 'Let's go, girls.'"

As we approach the entrance, I watch James and the beautiful woman beside him walk into the bar just feet away from me. I need a shot and someone else to think about for a little bit.

After grabbing a shot and a cocktail, I shimmy my way onto the packed dance floor. Swaying with the music, I fall into a trance, my mind replaying all the days and nights wrapped up in James' arms and sheets. The movie playing in my mind is stunning until my mind replaces me with the girl he was just holding on to outside. With my mind in panic mode, I come back to reality just to be slapped with a different kind of panic that I can't hide.

Sandy looks over her shoulder to find Jayden. "Oh, hello."

I feel the tightening in my chest, my pulse is rising, breaths getting shallow. *Snap out of it, Avery. Sandy needs you present right the fuck now.*

"Sorry, man, we were just heading out. Maybe some other time," I say after squeezing between Sandy and Jayden.

Rushing out the door, I feel Sandy fall in front of me and try to pull her back up, but we are struggling. James is just next door. I know that if I need him, he will come. Even if it's for Sandy and not me, I know he would save us.

"Here, let me help you," Jayden says before picking Sandy up.

I am fumbling around in my little purse to find my keys and phone. I find my keys first and unlock the Jeep, throwing the passenger door open while I continue searching for my phone. Sandy thanks Jayden and tries to shut the door, but he blocks it.

"Look, I know that what happened that night was scary, but I think that you were drugged and recently, someone else that I know was drugged there as well. Take this, it's the card for the detective that my cousin is talking to about what happened to her. If you remember anything from that night, just reach out to him, please."

I zone out for the rest of their exchange, phone in hand, with James' contact information pulled up in case I have to call him. When Sandy's door closes, I back up and leave the parking lot. Not only do I need space from what just happened, but I need the distance between me and James. I pull into a surf shop parking lot to get a clear head before continuing home.

"Do you believe him?" I ask

"I mean, this looks like a legitimate detective's card. What if it wasn't him that drugged me? What if this whole time I was accusing him and he was innocent? Since I declined to report what happened, I know that no one outside of us and Reed knows who I thought it was, but it still makes me feel bad now."

I nod. "Ok, we are not going to mentally unpack all of that tonight. Let's practice Memaw's mantra and sleep on that one. Let's get you to a doctor to check out your ankle."

I say as I reverse out of the parking spot I am in.

"Let's just go home. I don't think it's serious, just a

sprain. If it feels worse tomorrow, I will hit an urgent care.

Also, I say we keep running into Jayden between us, at least

until I decide if I'm going to talk to this detective. No

reason to worry Reed if there is nothing to worry about,"

Sandy says.

For the rest of our ride home, I mull over how I

felt seeing James tonight. By the time Sandy is settled in her

make-shift room and I have made my way to mine, I feel

like my heart has fractured so much that it will undoubtedly

shatter.

I reach around blindly under my bed to find Lucy.

"Get your furry little ass out here, ma'am. I need to talk to

you. I saw him and I am not okay. Why are you hiding from

me?" I whisper yell at her.

My hand meets fur and a soft fabric, I grab Lucy,

and she hisses at me the whole way out from under my bed.

"What has your fur in a twist?" I reach under the bed to

where she had been laying and pull out what she had always

been running to under there.

I hold the shirt up. "Lucy Elizabeth! You traitor

hussy! You have been hiding his missing shirt? I thought I

had issues over him, but obviously, yours are worse than

mine!"

I throw the shirt on the pillow next to mine and

watch Lucy curl up in a ball onto it and begin kneading the

shirt like it's dough. "I know, girl, I miss him too," I

whisper to her.

******

The next morning, Sandy and I decide to abandon

our original plans for a beach day and opt for a Rom Coms

of the 2000s movie marathon, complete with snacks of

every woman's diet nightmares: veggie tray, cracker and

cheese tray, chocolates, chips, ice cold cokes in a glass bottle, popcorn, and cookies.

In between movies, I turn to Sandy. "So, I think I am going to do the Costa Rica trip I mentioned. I think it might help me heal. Would you mind keeping an eye on Lucy Fur while I am gone?"

"Are you kidding me? Of course I will watch her, Aves, you don't even have to ask," she says turning to face me.

"Ok, I think I am going to go the last week of September and I will come home the week of Halloween. Is that ok?"

Sandy squeezes my hand. "Of course. Are you ready to talk about it all?"

I shake my head. "Not specifics. Long story short, I ended up getting serious with a customer. I know it was dumb to do, but you know how it goes. You spend enough time with them, you can't stop the connection that happens.

I let my guard down a little too much. We had a little argument and he said some things that hurt, super below the belt on low-rise jeans type shit. I need distance from him to help clear my head."

"You know, Aves, I will always be here when you are ready to open up. No matter where I am, I will always have time for you and not just the happy you. The sad you, too."

I can't help but smile. "Even when we are old and rolling through the nursing home in our glitzed-out wheelchairs? When I can't speak at a normal decibel and I scream a little?"

Sandy smiles back at me. "If you are too loud, I will adjust my hearing aid, but I will still be here then and on after that."

I grab Sandy's hand and curl up against the back of the couch after pressing play on our next movie. I am glad I have her here beside me. Even though I have not explained the whole scope of my situation, she stands beside me the same either way. I wish I had her unwavering trust. I suppose with her and her alone, I do. I was getting to that point with James; I was so close to that point with him. I focus back on the movie to stop the spiraling thoughts of him.

******

The weeks leading up to my flight were filled with making lists of places I want to see, shopping with Cal in our spare time to find cute outfits, hoarding as much time with Sandy as I can, and getting drinks with Brad when Sandy was occupied. I introduce Keri to Beth so that Keri can sit with Theo while I am gone. Keri said she needed something to keep her from spending money at the bars, and Beth said that if I trust her, she would too. I passed that detective's information to Keri for her to give to her cousin Talia. I never asked what came from her experience since she and I were not super close and I didn't want to pry, but I want to help her in any way I can.

"I can't believe you are leaving me for a whole month," Brad says as we pull in to Reed's driveway.

I look out the window in the opposite direction of the path that James and I took so many times before. "I think you will survive. Who knows, maybe with me gone, you will finally ask out that nurse at your school that you have the hots for."

Brad chuckles. "I already told you, Avey Davey, I do not stick my pen in company ink."

"I'm not saying to stick your pen anywhere. I am telling you to take the thermometer out of your ass and ask her on a proper date."

Brad shakes his head. "She may be hot and give off the naughty nurse vibes, but it won't happen. Besides, I heard her mention that she plans to put in her resignation around Christmas. Something about her fiancé's new job or something."

I shrug. "Ariana doesn't care about rings, why should you?"

Brad parks and cracks his knuckles. "Speaking of Ariana, we still haven't settled the whistle note queen debate."

******

My going-away dinner was catered by my favorite chef, Keri's cousin, Tasha. One of the few people added to my small list that I trust with my food, though I am forcing myself to expand the list. Reed was very kind to throw together this little shindig, but thanks to our secret love song, I am stuck across the table from James for this soiree.

Chris turns to me after she finishes her meal. "So, what made you decide to go to Costa Rica?"

I lean back in my seat while playing with Lola's hair. "Long story short, I gave someone too much of me and it blew up in my face, so I am going on a personal retreat."

"Seems extreme if you ask me," James says quietly with a scowl on his face, eyes locked on my necklace.

Out of habit, I play with the turtle pendant. "How does the saying go, James? 'Extreme times call for extreme measures,' I believe."

Brad pushes back from the table. "Oh, take a look at that: the sun is starting to set. Let's get the fire pit going or we will be missing out on my epic s'mores making tonight."

Lola and I stand to follow Brad as Sandy offers to stay back and clean. Brad has Lola on his shoulders with his arms full of s'mores necessities as we leave the kitchen and head out the back door. As soon as I step over the threshold, I am yanked around to the side of the house.

"Do you really think it is safe for you to travel to a foreign country alone?" James asks in a gruff whisper.

I shrug. "People do it every day."

James rubs his hand over his face. "Yeah, and women get trafficked every single day, Avery. I can't help but worry about you."

I pat James' shoulders. "Save your worrying for your new girlfriend, James. Don't waste it on me."

"My new girlfriend?" James asks.

I roll my eyes. "Don't play dumb, I saw the two of you at the pub. The pretty woman with the blondish brown hair. Save all your worrying for her, I don't need it."

James runs his hands through his hair and tugs on it. "She is not my girlfriend, Avery. She is a friend."

I let out a soft chuckle. "I know how you are with your friends, remember?"

James shakes his head. "You know what, just do what you want, Avery. You always do anyway."

"I plan to," I say over my shoulder as I walk towards Brad, Chris, and Lola.

Within two hours, Lola has fallen asleep on my lap, Chris has gone home, Reed and Sandy keep making sexy eyes at each other, Brad and James have been talking sports, and I have been sitting here trying to hold my emotions in. All I want to do is to run and jump into James's arms, apologize for being so childish and beg him to take me back.

******

"Avey Davey, wake up, sweet cheeks. Unless you want to skip Costa Rica and stay here. I won't complain if you do. Then I won't have to be the third wheel with Reed and Sandy Dandy for the next month," Brad says from my bedroom door.

I roll over and cover my nearly naked body with my sheet. "What time is it? Why didn't my alarm go off?"

Brad looks at his watch. "We have four hours until your flight leaves. As for your alarm, I have no idea, Davey. Go get ready, I'll start calling your phone and try to find it."

I stand up in my sheet dress. "I will only be like five minutes."

Brad pushes me towards the bathroom. "Take ten because you reek of a smoke pit and booze."

I take a quick shower. I don't even bother to shave my legs since I am wearing leggings on the flight. Opting to let my hair air-dry, I brush my teeth, throw on some deodorant, and throw my shower items in my carry-on bag.

"Any luck?" I yell from the bathroom.

"Nope, can't find it anywhere. I even checked my truck. Where do you last remember having it?" he asks.

I shrug. "Last night is a blur after leaving Reed's, and I don't remember when I last saw it there either. I think Lola was playing with it, but I could have sworn I put it in my pocket after that."

Brad shakes his head. "You are never allowed to start a drinking game at a bar with strangers again. Actually, you just aren't allowed to start drinking games, period. I haven't drank that much since college."

"If you can't hang with the baddies, stay on the stools with the saddies, Braddy," I tease. "I don't have time for a wild phone chase, so let's just stop by the store and I will get a temporary prepaid one. I will call Sandy, and if it is at Reed's, she can hold on to the old one for me."

Chapter 29
James

Sitting across the dinner table from Avery watching her carry on conversations with Sandy, Chris, and even Lola is absolute torture. I keep making small talk with Reed and Brad, but I can't get into anything that requires any thought because I can't keep my eyes or thoughts off of my Little Dove. We should be sitting here side by side. My arm should be draped around her shoulder while she leans into me and we laugh at something funny that Lola said. Our friends should be asking us when we will finally move in together or pestering me about when I will finally propose to her. Instead, I am sitting across from her, barely holding myself together as we collectively wish her good luck on her trip.

"So, what made you decide to go to Costa Rica?" Chris asks.

"Long story short, I gave someone too much of me and it blew up in my face, so I am going on a personal retreat," Avery responds.

"Seems extreme if you ask me," I say, my eyes drawn to the necklace I gave her still hanging around her neck. If she hated me, she wouldn't still be wearing it. She would have thrown it in the trash or something... Right?

"How does the saying go, James? 'Extreme times call for extreme measures,' I believe," she says.

Those were the same words I said to her the day we had our first kiss. She knew I would remember those words.

Brad pushes back from the table. "Oh, take a look at that: the sun is starting to set. Let's get the fire pit going or we will be missing out on my epic s'mores making tonight."

I stand and rush out of the back door while everyone else is taking their sweet time. When Avery finally walks out, I grab her arm and pull her around to the side of the house for some privacy.

"Do you really think it is safe for you to travel to a foreign country alone?" I ask. I am trying to whisper, but even to my own ears, I sound angry.

"People do it every day," she says, like it's nothing to be concerned about.

I frustratedly rub my face. "Yeah, and women get trafficked every single day, Avery. I can't help but worry about you."

"Save your worrying for your new girlfriend, James. Don't waste it on me," she says with a pat to my shoulders.

"My new girlfriend?" I ask, confused.

"Don't play dumb, I saw the two of you at the pub. The pretty woman with the blondish brown hair. Save all your worrying for her, I don't need it."

For fucks sake. I grab my hair. "She is not my girlfriend, Avery. She is a friend."

Avery laughs. "I know how you are with your friends, remember?"

She is not receptive to having a serious conversation right now. I am only going to make things worse. "You know what, just do what you want, Avery. You always do anyway," I say defeatedly.

"I plan to," she says as she walks away from me.

I stand there for a moment to gather myself. Every ounce of me wants to throw her over my shoulder, march her into my house and hash this out. I am so tired of staying away from her. I have to remind myself of why we are in this predicament today and that I wouldn't want Jack to be in the position I was in, so I won't allow myself to be either.

******

I am walking through the garage when Reed stops me. "Hey, you haven't happened to find a phone lying around, have you?"

I shake my head. "Nope. Who is missing one?"

"Avery. She doesn't know if she lost it here or at the bar that she and Brad went to when they left here. If you happen to run across it, will you give it to Sandy?"

I nod. "Yeah, of course I will. Did she leave on her trip with no cell phone?"

Reed shakes his head. "No, I guess they stopped at a store and got a replacement phone before her flight."

"Okay, that's good. I will keep my eyes open and if I come across it, I will give it to Sandy," I say.

"Thanks. Oh, Sandy and I will be back late tonight. I am finally going to ask her to move in over dinner," Reed says nervously.

I give Reed a side hug. "Look at my wittle man, growing up so fast."

Reed laughs and pushes me away. "Shut up, old man."

I laugh out, "You know, your parents would have loved her. Maybe we can convince Betty and her kids to come out to visit soon so Betty can meet her."

Reed nods. "Yeah, we should. I plan on asking her to marry me on her birthday. She told me how her ex would always make plans and then cancel them on her birthday. I planned to take her home and get her Memaw's and Uncle's blessing and surprising her then."

I pat his shoulders. "I think that is a great idea. She already feels like part of the family; we all love her and want her here."

Reed shakes his head in disbelief. "I know, I couldn't imagine this house without her anymore. It is like she was what was missing for so long."

I nod. "I agree. I have something to get to. Call me if you need me."

Reed chuckles. "A date. You have a date, James. It is okay to say the word."

I get in my car and flip Reed off. I can hear his laughter over the engine as I back out of my spot.

******

"Are you sure you are okay?" Dottie asks, playing with the hair at the nape of my neck.

I swallow the popcorn in my mouth. "Yeah, why do you ask?"

Dottie faces me fully. "You were putting so much popcorn in your mouth that I was worried you were going to choke. You should breathe between handfuls." She shakes the half-empty bag of popcorn in my lap.

"I am just hungry, I guess. I probably should have had a real lunch instead of just a protein shake earlier."

She rubs my neck again. "You know, we are both adults here. You can talk to me."

I drop my head and sigh. "I do know that. My ex left for a trip last week so she could put distance between us, and I am still working through everything in my own head."

Dottie hums. "I see. Is this the same ex that had you sulking in Chicago?"

I whip my head to her. "I was not sulking."

Dottie softly laughs. "You looked like someone killed your goldfish! That is why I sat beside you. You looked like you needed someone; a shoulder, a hug, a listening ear, something. The nurse in me was drawn to the hurting in you, I guess."

I huff out a laugh. "I guess you are right. Yes, I was sad then. We split a couple of days prior to that. I know it has been a while, and I should be over it, but for some reason, it is still weighing on me."

"You love her still?" Dottie asks, not accusing me, but truly asking because she cares.

I nod. "Yeah. I think I always loved her more than she loved me, though. You know how it is: the one who loves the most is the one who will hurt the most."

Dottie shakes her head. "I don't know how that is. My husband loved me deeply, probably more than I loved him at some points. It always evened out, though. Some days I loved him more than he did me and vice versa."

I am saved by the movie starting. I lean in towards Dottie and kiss her forehead. "I am glad you had someone who loved you so much."

She squeezes my hand and then leans her head against my shoulder for the movie.

Chapter 30
Avery

"I haven't even been gone a full week and you are already moving on? Peach, how could you? Ya know what, scratch that. You told me how good the sex is. You go girl! I am so excited for you."

"I know, I couldn't believe it," Sandy says, wiping her hand across her forehead to push her hair back.

I point to her hair on the video chat. "Peach, what in the hell are you doing?"

Sandy lets out a low curse after looking at the paint on her hand. "Damn, I think Lola would do a better job painting this monstrosity than I am. I am at your place working on her Halloween costume. It is weird to call it your place now."

I place my hand over my heart. "You know that your cute little ass will always be welcome. It will always still be your home too, Peach."

Sandy nods. "I know. Besides, we will still need our girls' nights in. I will just cuddle you on those nights."

I laugh. "Only if we put up a pillow wall. When we had our living room sleepover on the blow-up mattress, I woke up in the middle of the night with you gripping my boobs. Never mind, forget the pillow wall, that's the last time my boobs saw any action that wasn't from my own hands."

Sandy laughs. "Oh my word, I didn't even know I did that."

"No worries. Hey, did you ever happen to find my phone? I am really hoping I lost it at your place and not at the bar."

Sandy shakes her head. "No, I have searched Lola's room, her bathroom, outside in the yard, the downstairs bathroom. Reed and I told James to keep an eye out for it while he does his perimeter checks."

I have to force my face to stay neutral hearing his name. "Damn, I will just consider it a loss. I gotta run, I am meeting up with a couple of girls I met at the market today. Give Lucy kisses for me. I love you, Peach."

"I will, I love you too. Be safe and don't replace me."

After ending our video chat, I call my old phone number, hoping someone will answer it. Who am I kidding? I am hoping James will answer it. That the universe has my back and that he found my phone and is holding on to it until I get home so he has an excuse to see me. "Hey, you have reached my voicemail. If I wanted to talk to you, I would have answered, so don't waste our time. Just text me. K. Byyyeeeee." I roll my eyes at myself. Why did I think that was cute? Lesson learned, I suppose.

I throw myself back on the couch with a sigh. This trip was supposed to be my mental escape from him and here I am again: James Michael Sullivan front and center of every thought. Everywhere I went this past week, all I could think about was how much he would have enjoyed the volcano tour, the restaurant, and the ATV ride through the jungle. Why can my brain not shut him out completely like I need it to?

I notice the time, force myself to get off the couch, and jump into the shower. I met some girls today who told me about this hotel and casino that is supposed to be a nightlife hot spot. What better way to get my mind off of him than booze, bright lights, some gambling, and music on the beach?

******

A few hours later, we are being dropped off at the hotel. Sofia and I walk around while Isabella goes to check us into a room for the night. We figured we would be responsible adults and since we plan to drink until we can't walk, we will drink until we can still crawl to our room.

"Am I overdressed?" I ask Sofia, looking down at my long, billowy, cotton dress with a bikini underneath.

Sofia shakes her head and with her Spanish accent that I love so much says, "No amiga. You look, ummm, guapa, beautiful."

"Are you sure? Most of the women in here are wearing hardly anything. I feel a little uncomfortable, actually."

Sofia waves a hand in the air. "No mae, they are prostitutas."

I whip my head to Sofia and whisper, "Prostitutes?"

Sofia nods. "Si."

I look around now with my rose-colored glasses off and realize she is not kidding. There are tons of very young women here on the arms of much older gentlemen. Every time a man walks up to the bar, I see a swarm of women surround him until he walks away with one or more of them. I am glad James is not with me now; I would have been clawing apart any woman who walked too close to him.

Isabella comes up behind us waving around our key cards before handing us each one. "I am going to go check out our room and then hit the pool and bar. What about you two?"

Sofia shrugs. "Birra then pool."

Both girls look at me. "I think I am going to check out the casino first. I will meet y'all out at the pool in a bit."

Isabella cocks her head to the side. "Just be careful, okay? A lot of guys come here because of the easy access," she says, looking around at the women-to-men ratio. "Keep your head on a swivel."

I nod. "Coming in loud and clear. I will. Catch y'all in a bit."

Sofia grabs my hand. "Hasta luego, chica."

"Hasta luego," I respond.

I find a machine and get lost in the slots until I smell someone beside me. Literally smell him standing there. I turn slowly to face the gentleman with the overpowering cheap cologne.

"Hola, señorita," he says in a Spanish accent so bad that even I find it offensive.

"Hi," I say dryly.

"Oh, you speak English?" he asks.

I look at him in disbelief. "Obviously. Can I help you?"

He looks over my body. "I sure hope so."

I know that disgust is written all over my face. "I am pretty positive that I can't. Good luck on your hunt for the not-so-holy grail." I say, turning back to my slot machine.

Sir Stinks-a-lot slides his hand down my shoulder and arm. "Don't be like that, beautiful."

I smack his hand away. "This will be your one and only warning: Do. Not. Touch. Me."

Sir Stinks-a-lot goes to try to touch my shoulder again and before I can react, a large masculine hand grips his, twisting his wrist back.

"What the fuck, man," Sir Stinks-a-lot whines, pulling his hand to his chest to cradle it.

I turn to find a young, handsome guy standing behind my chair. "She told you that it was your one and only warning. You chose not to believe her."

"Fuck this," Sir Stinks-a-lot says as he turns to walk away.

I look up at my tan knight behind me. "Thank you. That guy really wasn't picking up what I was throwing down."

"Most visitors have a gross misconception of what is and isn't allowed here. Sorry about his ignorance. I am

Mateo. If he bothers you again, come find me. I will be behind one of the bars all night."

I nod. "Thank you, Mateo."

After Mateo walked away, I went to find Isabella and Sofia and let them know that I was going to head back to my rented temporary home for the month.

******

After spending a few nights alone in my temporary home, I decided to meet up with Isabella at a local bar for some drinks and a fun but relaxing night out. The bar has a super fun atmosphere; games to play, the music is upbeat but not deafening, and the crowd is a happy one. Isabella and I make our way to the bar to order our beers and a familiar face catches my eye.

"Fancy seeing you here," I say.

Mateo's smile widens when he recognizes me. "Did you lure any more poor men to meet their embarrassing rejection from you tonight?"

I shake my head and let out a soft laugh. "No, just Isabella."

Mateo looks at Isabella. "Hey, Cuz. Didn't think you would be making it out tonight."

I look between Isabella and Mateo.

Isabella shrugs her shoulders. "Felt like people watching. Pop some tops for us. First round is on you." Isabella turns to me. "Drink preference?"

I shake my head. "Anything bottled and light."

Mateo reaches down below the bar and sets two beers on the counter before opening them. "You two behave tonight, I don't want to have to break any hands again," Mateo says with a wink before walking to the other end of the bar to serve a group of giggling women.

I turn to Isabella. "Your cousin? He works here, too?"

Isabella takes a drink of her beer and then nods her head. "Yes, he works at both part-time so when I want to go drinking, I just go wherever he is. I have seen too much happen to good people, so I would rather drink where someone I know is watching out for me. Paranoid or prophetic, I just have this feeling that someday I will need him to be there for me."

A shiver run down my arms. "Definitely not paranoid. I get it."

******

I am sitting at the bar watching Isabella play an intense, yet flirtatious game of pool when I hear Mateo say, "She is going easy on him."

I look to Mateo. "Is she?" I ask.

He nods. "Absolutely, she always goes easy on the first game or if she thinks the guy is cute."

I take a swig of my beer. "Must be the first game then."

Mateo throws his head back with a laugh. "You don't think he is cute?"

I shake my head. "Not my type."

Mateo leans across the bar. "And what is your type?"

I shrug. "I don't think I know. I have only been with one person, so I don't think I have enough of a pattern built to know."

Mateo nods his head. "And where is he?"

I shrug again. "Probably with his really pretty new girlfriend back home."

Mateo's eyes soften. "Your face is not as pretty when you frown, and I enjoyed having something pretty to look at from this side. Pick a shot, on me."

I manage a half smile. "I really hope that is not your go-to pick up line because if so, you desperately need help."

Mateo snarls one side of his lip up. "You think I need pick up lines? ¡Dios mio!"

I giggle.

Mateo smiles. "There we go. So, tell me about this guy after telling me what shot we are taking."

I look to the spirits behind him. "Which rum is your favorite?"

Mateo nods his head. "I have got just the one."

*****

After a few shots, my long story about James and how everything went wrong, Isabella whooping that guy's ass three times at pool, followed by more drinks, and Isabella and I singing at the top of our lungs, Mateo guides us to his old beat-up truck after closing the bar.

"I am staying at your house tonight. Papa will kick my ass if I wake him up this late," Isabella squeaks out between hiccups.

Mateo rolls his eyes. "Fine, what about you?"

I point in the direction that I think we need to be going. "My rental is that way… I think. Actually, I don't know. Let me find the reservation info in my email so you can find it."

After fumbling through my phone for a few minutes, I find the email that has the address on it and pass my phone to Mateo. With a nod, he hands my phone back to me, and then pulls out onto the road. Within seconds, Isabella is leaning against Mateo, snoring.

I look over at her and giggle at the sight.

Mateo says softly, "It has been a long time since she felt comfortable around someone else to be this vulnerable. She didn't always have good friends around her. I am glad that she found you, uhm, I still don't know your name."

"Avery, Avery Jones." I play with my hands in my lap. "I know all too well how that can change you. I am glad we met. It's a funny story: I was lost, trying to find my rental after going to the market to get some food. I was freaking out that I couldn't find the house because I was so sure that I was on the right road. I ran into her, literally, and my bag split open, fruit and vegetables going everywhere. Long story short, I turned one street too early. She walked me to my place and we talked about what it is like to live here compared to America. I am lucky to have run into her that day."

Mateo turns onto my street and parks in front of my house. "It was nice to officially meet you, Avery. I hope to see you around. Stay safe."

"Thank you for tonight, Mateo, it was nice to have someone to talk to about my messed-up life who isn't directly involved with it daily."

Mateo taps his steering wheel with his thumb. "You know, it sounds like he really loved you, and that doesn't just go away. Maybe you should reach out to him. Set up a date at that coffee shop where you two would meet at. Neutral ground, you know. Maybe if you opened up to him, it could change things."

I nod and chew on my bottom lip. "Maybe. I have another week and a half here, so I still have some time to figure out what to do."

******

"Where is that damn phone? Hold on, don't hang up. I am trying to find you," I sing song to my phone that I keep misplacing. I have torn the couch apart by the time I find it sitting on the top of the back pillow.

"Hey, Butt Munch, why are you calling me during school hours?" I ask when I finally answer Brad's video chat.

"Sandy is in jail; how soon can you make it home?" he asks.

I roll my eyes and drop to sit on the floor after seeing the lack of available flights. "Hold on, let me look. The soonest flight I can find is for Monday. Just booked it. What happened?"

Brad shakes his head. "No idea. I will call you when I have more info."

I can feel the tears coming but keep my voice steady, hoping he can't see that I'm about to break down. No, not break down... shatter. "Ok, tell her I love her, and I will be there as soon as I can."

Brad is grabbing his keys and personal items off his desk. "She can hear you. Just get home when you can."

Brad hangs up and I let the tears fall freely. What could have possibly happened that would have led to Sandy, of all people, being arrested? I am kicking myself in the ass for not asking Brad for James' number right now. He would know what was going on.

I pull up the weather app and glare at the tropical depression moving in on Costa Rica right now. "You and I are feeling the same right now, storm. Furious and a mess, guaranteed to leave heartache in our wake. Though I do wish you would have waited just a little longer to make your way here so I could get to my best friend faster," I say to

the weather app on my phone staring back at me.

Chapter 31
James

It's a few days before Halloween; Chris has handed out costumes, and Sandy has been working on Lola's costume at Avery's house. I wait for Sandy to leave before sneaking over to the main house and tiptoeing into Lola's room to find Lucy Fur.

I know how much Lola loves this cat, but I also know this cat is obsessed with me. Every other day, I sneak in here to rub Lola's stuffed animals all over me so they hold my scent and Lucy will stay in here with Lola. I have had to chase that damned cat down multiple times during the day when I have walked out the back door to head home. Avery would be crushed if anything happened to Lucy, so I have found this is an effective way to keep the cat in one area. I even threw one of my shirts between the mattress and footboard of Lola's bed so the cat will sleep on the bed with her every night.

I make my way downstairs before Sandy makes her way in from the garage.

"Do you want help getting that upstairs?" I ask her.

She drops the paper mâché Mystery Machine on the kitchen floor. "Thanks, but I've got it. I'm going to go hide it upstairs in my storage room before Lola gets home."

I grab a bottled water from the fridge. "Good call. Otherwise, she would fight to sleep in it every night between now and Halloween."

Sandy pushes her hair back off her face. "Yes, she would. And since we are all suckers for her charm, no one in this house would tell her no."

I laugh. "You are absolutely right. That little girl runs this house and we are just here to serve her."

Sandy nods. "The princess, indeed."

I tip my water bottle towards Sandy. "I am heading to do a second workout. You know where I will be if you need me."

Sandy picks up her project. "Will do, don't kill yourself in that gym. I don't know what's wrong, but I can tell something is going on in your world. I am here if you need a place to vent."

I place a hand on her shoulder. "I appreciate it, Sandy. Reed is lucky to have found you."

Sandy pats my hand. "He is, isn't he?"

*****

After my workout and a shower, I make my way to my desk and wake the computer screens up in time to see a line of cop cars driving out of the front gate. I put some clothes on and take the golf cart over to the main house to find out what is going on. Before I make it all the way to the house, Reed is walking out the back door.

I jump out of the golf cart. "What the hell just happened?"

Quietly, Reed says, "Sandy was arrested for abusing Lola."

I follow his eyes and see Gina standing in the dining room window. "Shut the fuck up."

Reed looks at me in shock. "What?"

I cross my arms. "You heard me. There is no way that Sandy has been abusing Lola."

Reed shakes his head. "James, I have seen bruises on her and Gina has pictures of others. I know you don't want to believe it, but it is true."

I stomp towards the house. "Show me."

Reed grabs the pictures and we go to his office. Thumbing through the pictures, some of these bruises look familiar. One of them, I know for a fact, was from when she fell while playing in the backyard with Sandy because we laughed later that day about how the rock she fell against made a heart-shaped bruise and Lola said it's because the rock must love her. Another one looks like the one she got after falling off her bike; her elbow was scraped from that fall as well. When I asked her if she needed a popsicle after bandaging it, she told me no because she has superpowers and her skin grows back on its own, so she doesn't need the medicine from popsicles to make it heal.

"Can I take these over to my place?" I ask.

Reed nods. "Go right ahead, I can't look at them anymore."

Flipping through the pictures again, I ask, "What has Lola said about all of this? Did she confirm that these came from Sandy?"

Reed shakes his head again. "No, Gina said not to pressure her."

I let out a husky laugh. "Of course she did. See ya later." I don't even give Reed a chance to respond as I rush to the golf cart to head back over to my place. I know that I have videos to show that most of these are from true accidents.

******

I glance at the corner of the computer screen to see that I have been at my computer for multiple hours. Just past one, I stand and stretch to relieve the stiffness from sitting at this computer for so long. I pull up the live camera feed and see Gina rushing out of the front door and getting into her car in the circle drive in front of the house. I shake my head while muttering curses under my breath. She was awful to Reed when they were married, and I can see that she is just as wretched now.

******

I make my way over to the main house after I spent my entire Saturday printing screenshots and making sure I went through every video of Lola playing outside since Sandy began working for us. I decided that I would bring a little routine back to this house to try to hold this family together.

I am in the kitchen making pancakes with Lola sitting on the counter beside me, dancing along to one of Sandy's favorite songs. It is catchy and I can't help but dance along with it.

"Daddy, can I twy out my codtume today? I found it wadt night." Lola asks.

Reed walks to the coffee pot. "Of course, we will try it out after breakfast. What is all of this?"

I put the last pancake on a plate and turn to Reed. Smugly, I say, "Oh, well, Sir, that is the paperwork that I am taking to the judge in the morning to get Miss Darling's charges dropped. Feel free to take a look."

Reed studies the pictures for a few minutes. "Ok, this explains some. Princess, what happened to you to get the rest of these bruises you have had?"

Lola looks at her dad. "I awweady towd you, Daddy, nuffing."

Reed hides his frustration and calmly says, "Bruises don't just appear without you getting hurt, honey."

Lola smiles. "Yeah dey do, Daddy. Mommy dowwed me."

I knew Gina had something to do with all of this.

"Will you show Daddy how?" Reed asks.

Reed helps Lola off the counter, and she walks to Reed's bathroom where she opens a drawer that contains Sandy's makeup. She pulls out a few different things.

"Hewe, give me yow, awm daddy, I dow you how mommy dood it," Lola says, readying her supplies in front of her.

I thrust my arm out. "Daddy has a phone call to make, Princess. Do it on me instead."

I watch in amazement as this little four-year-old girl uses these different make-up products to create a realistic-looking bruise on my arm. Reed wasted no time running to find his phone.

******

I am watching Reed pace in front of the door outside the jail where we were directed to wait. He wanted to come alone this morning, but I convinced him to let me drive so that he and Sandy could talk in the back. The door creaks open and my stomach turns when I see Sandy walk out. She is bruised from head to toe, split lip, and limping on one foot, which I can tell from here is broken. She refuses to look at Reed and starts walking toward me. I instantly scoop her up into my arms, refusing to let her take even one more step on that broken ankle. I carry her to my car and put her in the back with all the ease that I can.

"To the hospital," Reed says from the back seat.

I nod and don't look at him. I want to blame him for the state Sandy is in right now, but I know the blame falls on Gina. I tried to call Avery on Friday, but she never answered my call, then I remembered that she lost her phone. I called Brad to see if he had talked to her, and he informed me that Sandy had called him from jail and that he had called Avery. She will be here in a few hours at most and he will be picking her up from the airport. At least he will be here with her.

After carrying Sandy into the emergency room, I came back out to the car to call Chris and let her know what was going on. She assured me that she would stay with Lola as long as we needed, and to focus on Sandy. While Sandy was in surgery, I sat with Reed in the waiting room. Both of us silent, neither of us ready to speak about the horrendous vision burned into our memories.

When the doctor came out to let us know that Sandy was in a room and could have visitors, I stayed back to wait for Avery and Brad while Reed went upstairs. I wanted to make sure to give Avery a heads up on what to expect before she walked in and saw Sandy.

"Hey man, how is she?" Brad asks when they walk through the double doors.

My eyes instantly find Avery. "She will be okay. It will take a lot of rest and therapy, but the surgery went well."

Avery's eyes widened. "Surgery? What the hell happened?"

I shrug. "I don't know what all happened. She didn't want to talk around Reed. You need to prepare yourself before you walk into that room. She took one hell of a beating, and it shows. But she is alive and from the looks of it, will heal with some time."

Avery grabs Brad's arm for support. Sandy found comfort in my arms, and Avery is finding hers in Brad's.

"Now that you two are here, I am going to head home to Lola. Call if you need anything. Chris will be staying at the main house tonight, too, so that I can run up here if you need anything," I say to Avery.

Brad nods to me. "Sounds good. I will drive Reed home when he is ready. Come on, Davey, let's go see our girl, huh?"

Avery lets Brad lead her toward the elevators, but pauses halfway down the hallway to turn and give me a nod. I wave my hand to her before dropping my head and turning to leave.

Chapter 32
Avery

There is no warning that could have prepared me for what I saw when I walked into Sandy's hospital room. Even with her facing the window, I can see the blue and purple on the side of her face that is visible to me, the bruises on her arm and neck. Her leg is elevated with a contraption holding it in the air.

"Holy fuck! What the fuck happened?" Anger dripping from every syllable, I turn my wrath to Reed, "You! You get the hell out of here! This is all your fucking fault! Go! Get! Now!" I am pointing to the door that Brad and I just walked in from. Willing myself to stand here. Willing myself to not jump on Reed and give him bruises and cuts to match Sandy. Lord knows he deserves them!

My head snaps up when the doctor walks in, and I hear Cal's voice. "Miss Darling, I am Doctor Campbell, one of the doctors who will be keeping an eye on you. Your surgery went well. We did have to put a couple of plates and some screws in, so you will have this boot on, and you can't put any weight on it for at least two weeks. I will see you around that time, and we will evaluate if you can then. In the meantime, we will get you some crutches. Normally, I would let you go home today, but with the broken rib and everything else your body has been put through, I want to keep you here for a couple of days to make sure we didn't miss any injuries." He pauses to look at the tablet in his hand. "I didn't notice any internal bleeding on the scans, but I want to repeat them in twenty-four hours to make sure." He looks at Sandy, giving her a sincere smile. "In the meantime, if you need anything, just hit the call light and we will try to make you as comfortable as possible."

Before Cal walks out, I notice the head nod to the door, telling me he will be waiting outside for me.

I turn to Sandy. "Peach, sweetie, I am here when you are ready to talk. Want me to put on a show? Read a book?"

Sandy shakes her head. "I just want some peace and quiet, if that is ok."

I nod. "Of course. I am going to go grab a coffee, want anything?"

Sandy shakes her head. I drop my own before heading out to the hallway to find Cal. I see him standing down at the end of the hallway by the stairs and make my way over to him.

He opens the door to the stairs and when we get into the stairwell, I turn to him and let my tears fall freely. "Will she be okay? Honestly?"

Cal hugs me with one arm while running his other hand over the back of my hair. "Physically, yes. I give you my word that everything that we have seen thus far will heal with time. Mentally and emotionally, that will be up to her. I swear to you that I looked over every scan myself when I saw her name, then had only the people that I trust the most look over it as well. I will keep an eye on every lab."

I nod against his chest. "Thank you so much!"

A throat clears behind me. I turn to see James staring at me with pain-filled eyes.

I pull back from Cal. "James, wait."

James shakes his head wordlessly and turns to jog down the stairs.

"Wait, James. Please?" I call to him.

James waves a hand behind him in the air, essentially waving me off.

I turn to face Cal. "Fuck," I whisper.

Cal opens one arm to me. "Let's go get you a coffee and then get you back up to Sandy's room. My treat."

I nod and let Cal lead me down the stairs where I just watched James run away from me.

******

The first couple of days with Sandy home took some trial and error, finding ways to work around the new setup and added equipment. I opted to sleep on the couch with her most nights. Lucy Fur enjoyed the pull-out couch more than Sandy or I did. I was scrolling through movies to pick our next adventure flick when I heard a knock at the front door. Sandy and I both glance at the door and then at each other.

"Are you expecting anyone?" Sandy asks me.

I shake my head. "Nope. If it were Brad, he would just use the key I gave him."

"If it is someone in a costume about to sing a telegram or something, send them to Brad's house," Sandy says with a laugh.

I giggle. "That would be comical."

I roll off the couch bed and stroll to the front door just to open it and freeze.

"No monologue about holding back the ferocious dog this time?" James asks.

I shake my head.

James pulls some flowers from behind his back. "I hope it is okay that I dropped by. I wanted to check on Sandy."

My heart drops, why did I think he was here for me? Idiot. I open the door all the way to allow him in. "Of course, come on in. Sandy, it's for you, but unfortunately, it doesn't sing."

Sandy glances back over the back of the couch. "Oh, thank goodness! Though I have heard James sing, and he has a lovely voice."

I raise an eyebrow. "Oh yeah?"

James shrugs.

"Yeah," Sandy continues, "what is that musical? The one with the guy who starts a circus, you know the one, Aves. It is a song from that one."

I look at James, and his eyes drop to the flowers he has extended towards Sandy. "Sandy, these are for you."

She grabs them and brings them to her nose to smell them. "They are beautiful. Thank you."

I walk around the couch bed. "Here, I will put those in some water and give you two some privacy."

It has been a while since I have felt the tightening in my chest like I am feeling now. I better not have a panic attack right now. *Get it together, me!* I lean against the counter and focus on even breathing. I can hear James and Sandy murmuring behind me, but their words sound like they are speaking underwater. *Breathe. Try to focus on hearing a word. Just one.* Gina. *You got one, Avery, let's try to hear two this time.* Lola. Lucy. *Good job, me! Now, try for as many as you can; you are almost out of this. You can do this.*

"… He doesn't know how. You know how us men are. We will always do the wrong thing, even when we are trying to do the right thing. Love makes us idiots," I hear James say.

There is some shuffling around and turn to see James giving Sandy a hug.

"Alright, well, I will leave you two ladies to enjoy the rest of your day. I just wanted to check in and see with my own eyes how you are doing."

Sandy turns to fully face James. "I am so glad that you did. I have missed you. Don't be a stranger."

James nods to Sandy. "Of course not. Good to see you again, Avery," he says to me.

I nod. "You too. I will walk you out."

*****

"Alrighty then, Lucy Fur, you be good for Uncle Brad. I will hide some catnip around the house for you tomorrow before we leave. Brad asked that you quit jumping out at him from the windowsill. He said you will be the cause of him having a heart attack someday, and we really need a solid babysitter for you. You keep running everyone off."

"Meoooooow"

"You can say it isn't your fault all you want, but I know the truth. Dobs still has a scar from that time I had to go help Mom drive from Virginia down to the Keys. Just play nice."

"Meeeeow"

"Yes, I am a little nervous about going to Texas again, but we are going to stay at Memaw's and I spent most of my childhood there, so I think I will be okay. I know how to pull myself out of a panic attack now and I had the doctor prescribe me some anti-anxiety pills just in case I need them in a pinch. Let's run through the checklist one more time to make sure I didn't forget anything."

Texas Checklist

- ☐ Girl power playlist

- ☐ Snacklebox

- ☐ Old Hollywood nighty and robe for me
- ☐ Old Hollywood nighty and robe for Sandy and Memaw
- ☐ Chill pills
- ☐ Clothes
- ☐ Toiletries

"Yep, looks about right, Lucy." Let's go check on Sandy. I turn and wave for Lucy to follow me into the living room, but she runs under my bed instead.

"Alright, Peach, all my stuff is packed, snacklebox for the trip is prepped with all of our favorite salty and sweet snacks, girl power playlist of the early 2000s complete. All we have to do is load it in the morning, and we are good to go. Oh, we should put the top down and recreate the Romy and Michelle scene. You know, the one of them trying to sing Footloose. I have always wanted to do that. I am going to find us some scarves to wear," I say, running back to my room.

I hear Sandy yell from the living room, "Avery, why are you calling me from your bedroom?"

What is she talking about? I hop into the living room with my hands on full display. "I'm not, Peach."

Sandy flips her phone to show my name calling her across her screen.

"OMFG, my old phone. Hurry, answer it. Someone found it," I urge.

"Hello?" Sandy looks at me with a confused look, "Lola? Lola, where did you find this phone, Sweetness?"

Chapter 33
James

"I'm coming," I say to my phone that is ringing before swiping accept on the call.

"Gina is in the trees between us. I don't know what she is doing here, but I just want to give you the heads-up," Reed says.

I turn to head to my office where my screens are to pull up the security cameras. "Do you want me to call Detective Roman?"

"Yeah. Knowing Gina, she is probably just here to beg me to drop everything or to help with damage control, but either way, ask him to come out so we can start the process to have her barred from here. I don't want her coming to this house ever again," he says.

"Got it, Boss. Holler if you need me," I say and then end the call.

I continue watching the monitors while I call Detective Roman.

"Detective Roman, how can I help you, James?" he asks.

"Hey, Detective, Gina is here. It is the oddest thing, she is running around through the tree line. Reed asked me to call and see if you would send someone out to start the process to bar her from coming here again."

"I can do that. Actually, if you can keep her there for about twenty minutes or so, I can come out myself," Detective Roman says.

I nod. "I am sure we can do that. See you soon."

I look down to hang up, and when I look at the screens again, my heart stops. Gina is pointing a gun at Reed and forcing him back into the house where we do not have cameras set up. I jump out of my seat and look around while I try to find an excuse to just walk into his house. Heading to the kitchen, I see the nearly empty container of pre-workout that I set out as a reminder to grab some more. That will work.

When I get to his back door, I take a deep breath and say a quick, silent prayer before walking in as calmly as possible. "Hey, Boss, thanks for letting me borrow this pre-workout. I like this one better than the one I have. Oh, hi Gina, what are you doing over this way?"

"James, you always did have impeccable timing," Gina says before pointing the gun at me. "You two, get to the table, now."

Reed and I both walk over to the table and I pick the chair that is closest to Gina to sit on. I am running through every possible escape and strategy to get us out of here, mostly unharmed, until Gina's phone rings. She continues her pacing when she answers. On the table, I write out Lola with my finger, hoping Reed will understand. He gives a slight nod and subtly points to the floor above us. Ok, I need to come up with a plan to get us and Lola out safely.

"…The judge we paid to keep Sandy in for the weekend is already paid for this, too. Shut up, Charles, it will all be fine. I worked it all out. Ok, talk to you later." Gina hangs up the phone.

"Gina, what is your end goal here?" Reed asks her.

Gina looks at Reed. "Is it not obvious?"

I lean forward. "I thought my eyes were playing tricks on me the other day when I saw you with a guy that looked like Charles." I turn to Reed. "The one that wanted your dad's legacy."

Gina flashes an insincere smile. "Though you're old, dear James, your eyes did not deceive you. We have been dating since the divorce. Mutual hate sure can bring two people together."

I lean back in my chair and shake my head. "You two are both sick people, so it is fitting."

Gina's smile grows wider. "Like I said, James, you always did have impeccable timing."

I fall to the ground, my head thumping off of it before I can even register what just happened. There was a crack, followed by pain, and then I was on the ground. I can see Reed's mouth moving. I see movement behind Gina and look to see Lola, she is talking but I can't make out any words. Her eyes find mine and I give her a look that I hope portrays to hide. Hide and don't come out. I watch her walk away and am relieved.

Reed and Gina keep going back and forth for what feels like an hour. Every now and again, I can make out a word or two, but for the most part, I feel like I am watching a silent movie around me. I can tell that I am close to losing too much blood. I am starting to feel cold and the pain from the gunshot isn't hurting as bad as it did. I see movement behind Gina again and am pretty sure I am hallucinating. Gina turns to face Reed's bedroom and starts walking towards it.

I grab Reed's arm. "Sandy is in the house," I whisper to him. A few seconds later, she is crouched beside me.

"Come on, Peter is just outside on the side of the house. Help me get him out the door," I hear her say.

They grab my arms and legs and move me out the back door to where Peter is waiting for me. The pain is unbelievable again, so I know I have a few more minutes at least.

Peter grabs under my arms and starts dragging me into the tree line. "Hang in there, my friend. You have a lovely young lady waiting at my house to see you. Well, two technically. Miss Avery is there with Lola."

I gasp out, "Tell her I love her, that I will watch over her. Will you?"

Peter chuckles. "In your dreams. She will kill me before I have the chance if she doesn't see you breathing when we get to my side of the fence. By the way, I found the hole. Lola showed me so I could get over here without being seen. She said to watch out for the wicked witch, though."

I sputter out a coughing laugh. "The only witch here is her mother, unfortunately. Just make sure my Dove knows that I love her. Please."

Two gunshots cut through the quiet. Peter startles, the pain takes over, and I fall into a void.

Chapter 34
Avery

I am pacing the hospital room for an entire hour before the monitor's beep pattern changes and pulls me from my own thoughts. Slowly, I turn and fall to the floor with relieved tears when I see his eyes looking back at me.

"Avery? What is going on?" James asks roughly.

I jump up and rush over to him. Placing my hand on his arm and trying to keep my voice steady, "Gina shot you, you had to have surgery. A doctor will come to explain everything shortly."

"Reed? Lola? Sandy?"

I shake my head, and the tears start falling again. "Lola is safe. She was with me, but is now with Chris. Sandy had her climb out of the window and run to Peter's house. Apparently, Lola and Sandy knew about the hole in the fence and called it the 'Witches Portal' during their games."

James huffs out a laugh. "She does have a great imagination. Reed and Sandy?"

I suck in a deep breath. "Reed is downstairs in the emergency department still. Last time I checked, the police were talking to him."

James grabs my hand. "Why do you keep avoiding talking about Sandy?"

I wipe the tears from my cheek. I open my mouth to try to tell him, but the only thing that comes out is a deep sob. Shaking my head, I look in his eyes and see the moment my silent answer registers for him.

James tries to move but winces from the pain and falls back against the bed. He runs his free hand down his face. "The cracks I heard before I passed out?"

I nod. "The coroner said it was instant and she did not suffer. There was nothing that could have saved her."

The tears begin falling down James' face. "Gina?"

I bite my lip for a second before responding, "When the police stormed inside, she shot herself. The gunshots were less than three seconds apart."

James opens his arms for me to cuddle into him, so I do. "I should have grabbed my gun. I was so worried about grabbing something to use as an excuse to walk in, that I didn't even think to grab one of my fucking guns."

I rub my hand soothingly over his cheeks. "Shhhhh. Don't even think about that now."

"I need to call Jack."

"I will run down stairs and check on Brad and Reed so you can have some privacy," I say into his chest.

James squeezes me tight. "Promise me you will come back up, Dove."

I gasp out a sob and lift my face to see his. "Only if you want me to."

James places both hands on either side of my cheeks. "I want you."

I nod my head in understanding. He doesn't just mean here physically. "I want you," I say back and lean in to kiss him when the door opens and a doctor walks in.

"Please excuse my lack of professionalism right now, but it is about damn time," Cal says.

James looks at Cal and then at me.

Cal extends a hand. "Doctor Calvin Campbell. Avery's very gay friend, but also one of your doctors. Unless you choose to have me replaced, in which case, I would totally understand and no hard feelings."

James looks at me again and I nod.

Cal straightens his jacket. "I will take that as I am here to stay as your doctor. Let's talk about your surgery, shall we?"

I stand. "I am going to go check on the other guys while you two have this talk, and so you can call Jack."

415

James grabs my hand and pulls me down for a kiss. "Don't be gone too long, I need your mending cuddles, obviously."

"They are magical, aren't they?" Cal butts in.

James and I glare at him and Cal puts his hands in the air.

"I'll be back soon. I promise." I walk out the door and head downstairs to find Brad and Reed.

Chapter 35
James

"Hey, Jack."

"Dad, hey! Good timing. I am stopped in Georgia, I still have a few hours left."

I rub a hand down my face. "Kiddo, something happened. Get a hotel when you get here, Reed's house isn't available anymore."

"What happened?"

"It's a long story. I was shot. Reed and Lola are fine, but Sandy was killed, and Gina committed suicide there. I doubt any of us will ever step foot in that house again. Find a hotel and I will give you my card when you get to town. I will text you my room number at the hospital. I will be here for a few days minimum."

"What the actual fuck?! Are you okay, Dad? What happened? Oh my god, I'm on my way!"

"Jack, stop. Breathe. I am alive. I had surgery and I will be okay with some antibiotics and physical therapy. Do not get back on that bike in a panic. Do you hear me?"

"You are right. I hear you. I just can't believe this happened!"

"I know, Kiddo. Trust me, I know."

"I will stay at a friend's house. Where are you going to stay? Reed and Lola?"

"I will figure it out for myself when I leave here. As far as Reed and Lola, I don't know yet. I haven't talked to Reed. Avery just went down to check on him."

"Avery? Was she there when this happened?"

"No, she was next door. I will tell you all the details when you get here. Just be present while you are on your bike, okay?"

"I know, Dad. I will probably hang out at this place I am at for a half hour or so to make sure the jitters and nerves are gone. I love you and I am glad you are okay!"

"I love you, too, kiddo. See you later."

I turn my head to face the door, hoping that Avery really does come back to my room. I am done letting pride or anything else stand between us. This morning was a wake-up call as to how short life really is, and I won't waste another second of her not being in mine.

The morphine is taking over when Avery walks in. "How are you feeling?"

I look around the room. "Like a man who was shot."

Avery's face falls. "No downplaying James. Not today, not ever about what happened today."

I reach out a hand for her. "I am sorry, Dove, I don't know how to navigate this right now."

Avery nods. "I understand, I don't either. I feel like a piece of shit, honestly."

"Why?" I ask.

Avery takes a step forward. "I lost my best friend today, and I have cried for her. I will cry for her many more times to come, I know this. But a part of me is so relieved to see that you are okay that I feel like an awful friend...that any part of me can be relieved right now."

I pull Avery down onto the bed with me. "You are not an awful friend, Dove. Sandy knows how much you love her and we will cry together for her many times to come, but she would understand you feeling conflicted because you have more than just her in your heart." I rub Avery's hair. "She was selfless and would be mad at you if you only thought about her and her alone. You know this."

Avery snorts out a giggle. "You are right, she really would be. I called her Memaw and Uncle. They want her funeral to be there, and they asked that all of us come out."

I nod. "Anything they want. Reed and I will cover all expenses. Let her know that."

"I did, Reed said that before you had a chance. He is a mess, James. They are going to go stay with Brad."

Avery looks up at me. "Where will you go?"

I shrug. "I haven't thought about it yet."

Avery nuzzles into my neck. "With me. You will come home with me. I can't be there alone."

I kiss her head. "You run this show."

Avery shakes her head. "I don't want to run it alone anymore."

"You will never be alone again, Dove."

Epilogue
Brad

I couldn't stand being in the same room as everyone any longer. Watching all these strangers with smiles on their faces telling us all how sorry they are for our loss was making me want to punch every single one of them in their fake ass faces. Outside of Reed, Lola, James, Avery, Sandy's Memaw, her Uncle Alex, Chris, and myself, no one shed a single tear for her today. There were a lot of dropped heads, but no tears from these people who did not deserve to mourn such a beautiful soul without paying the price of true grief for her absence.

With a bottle of whiskey, I am hiding out behind a gravestone at the town's only cemetery. I wanted to be close to Sandy, but I couldn't look at her headstone. Not yet. The last three weeks have been hell since the shooting. It feels a little morbid to be having Sandy's funeral on her birthday, but it is what her Memaw wanted and it gave enough time for her headstone to be made once Reed paid double the price to have it expedited.

I drop the bottle from my mouth when I hear Avery talking. I peek around the headstone I am leaning against to see her sitting beside the freshly shoveled dirt covering Sandy's eternal resting place. She is reading something to Sandy, shuffling the papers around in her hands. I can't make out the words, but I can see the heartache written across her face. She puts the pages down, wipes her tears and laughs before she starts talking again. I watch her lean over and kiss Sandy's headstone and the one beside hers before standing and walking to James, who was waiting by a tree for her. After a few steps he turns his head back, locks eyes with me, and jerks his head up with a nod. Looking at my watch, I see it is time for us to head to the small airport in town where our jet is waiting.

I stand and wipe the dirt off my pants, chug the rest of the whiskey in the bottle, and make my way to Sandy. I fall to my knees beside her, bow my head and let a few more tears fall. "I will try to help him, I promise I will. Just don't judge me for how I cope behind closed doors to do it."

Acknowledgements

I have to start my acknowledgements off with a big THANK YOU to my editor, Adi! I promise that someday I will make your job easier…not today, but someday. Thank you for cleaning up my mess.

Author Jessi Called, you are the best alpha reader a girl could ask for! I will forever be grateful that you take time out of your own hectic work and writing schedule to help make sure my story makes sense!

To all my Betas, your advice, guidance, suggestions, and grammatical finds truly help me more than you will ever know. You guys and gals are the best!

To my family, thank you for your help with the kids and all around support while I chase this dream of mine. I am beyond blessed for everything y'all do for me.

About The Author

Jannah is a stay-at-home mom who spends most days catering to little humans and her fur doggies. When she is not busy with housework, kids, or her geriatric dogs, she is writing, reading, or listening to books.

The only time she watches TV is during hockey season. GO CAPS!

If there were an award for being Murphy's Law Number One Target, she would own it.

Her favorite hobby is baking mass quantities of cookies to disperse to her physical therapists, tanning gals, and anyone else she feels needs a cookie hug at the time.

Want to keep up with the author, Brad, see what is next to come, or watch Jannah's Murphy's Law chronicles? Follow her on any of these socials.

Facebook: Author Jannah Jette

Instagram: @authorjannahjette

Tiktok: @author.jannah.jette

Email: jannahjettesocials@gmail.com

Want to see the Turtle painting Avery bought James? Check out Melissa Williams art at ViaMeliaArt.com. Sandy and James won't be the only one in this series who receives one of Melissa's paintings. Be on the lookout for the final book in The Three Shots Series, For Those Who Need Help To Feel to see what Brad buys!

Books In This Series
The Three Shots
Series

The Three Shots Series follows a group of friends turned family as they navigate through healing from their past and present trauma while finding love and loss along the way.

For Those Who Hurt- Sandy leaves her hometown after finding her boyfriend having an affair with his secretary. She is heading East to room with her best friend and is ready to start her new and improved life. Should she have stayed in her hometown?

For Those Who Heal- Avery found a lucrative way to kill two birds with one stone. One client flips Avery's life upside down and takes her on an emotional rollercoaster, forcing her to face past demons. Will she come out of this healed or brokenhearted?

For Those Who Need Help to Feel- Brad is struggling to keep up the facade that he is okay until a woman comes along who makes him feel again. Can he put aside his coping crutch in time to keep her, or is history doomed to repeat itself?